Billy's Search for the Healing Well

About the Author

Helen C Burke was born in Drogheda County Louth on 31st October 1955 and now lives in Kent with her husband. Passionate about writing she wrote *Billy's Search for the Healing Well*, her debut book, which had previously languished on her computer for five years, while travelling around Europe and Morocco. A mother of three adult children and grandmother of three, Helen worked as a part time Administration Assistant for her local Adult Education Authority before taking a career break to travel and improve her writing skills.

Helen C Burke

Billy's Search for the Healing Well

Cover Illustration by Simon P Murtagh

Olympia Publishers
London

www.olympiapublishers.com
OLYMPIA PAPERBACK EDITION

A CIP catalogue record for this title is
available from the British Library.

ISBN: 978-1-84897-761-7

This is a work of fiction.
Names, characters, places and incidents originate from the writer's
imagination. Any resemblance to actual persons, living or dead, is
purely coincidental.

First Published in 2017

Olympia Publishers
60 Cannon Street
London
EC4N 6NP

Printed in Great Britain by CMP (uk) Limited

Dedication

To my beautiful grandchildren, Ryan, Bridie & Elliott.
May you always be so well loved.
With love
Your Nana

Acknowledgments

I would like to thank my family for their support, for discussing the story, reading, and offering comments. Particularly, my husband, Richard, who, ever encouraging, made endless cups of tea.

I would like to acknowledge Glendalough, a magical place, in stunning County Wicklow, which I'm sure has inspired, and will continue to inspire many more stories to be written.

And of course, a big thank you to Olympia Publishers for giving me the opportunity to publish my first book.

I will be thrilled if you enjoy reading *Billy's Search for the Healing Well* as much as I have enjoyed writing it.

Introduction

Billy blinked through the porthole at the never-ending, steel grey sea disappearing over the horizon, and, heaving again, he splattered the wall. Scared, he looked around the strange bare room, where he'd woken on a hard wooden floor, with his blue hoody covering him… and still wearing his trainers? No wonder he prickled with pins and needles. Where was his dated Spiderman wallpaper and matching curtains, his bed, his bookshelves, his worn rug and wonky lamp? Looking up, he traced the chugging hissing, ugly pipes across the ceiling and down the wall, like a giant game of snakes and ladders. Was he dreaming? A memory came flooding back and a shiver ran down his spine. He had been running down a street in the dead of the night and ducking under a barrier at the port. Burying his head in his hands, he groaned aloud. Last night while his gran was sleeping, he'd run away. He was still on the ferry! Flicking up the lid of his 007 watch, he struggled to make out the digits, its novelty light turning his face a fluorescent green. Pressing his nose against the cold glass, he looked again. The ferry wasn't supposed to leave for another hour, and yet, it was bouncing across the Irish Sea leaving an angry trail of white foam. His stomach lurched and he heaved again, splattering the wall and his shoes with a fountain of spew. He'd meant to get off! Looking at his watch again, he saw that it had stopped.

Chapter 1

Billy's Gran

Billy wasn't sure why his mum was in hospital, but he was happy to stay with his gran. It meant he could hang around with Ginger Nick, and Jimmy and Emma, the twins from next door, for the whole of the summer holidays. Strange things happened at his gran's, who annoyingly called him William, because 'Billy', she said, reminded her of a bad-tempered goat. For a start, his gran made wedding dresses, prom dresses and christening gowns appear from her clunky, old sewing machine, faster than a magician could pull bunting from his sleeve. She painted weird fairies too, whom she called the meadowers – some pretty, some not, and some ugly, who winked at him from jumbled frames on the walls.

"Ah, that'll be the special paint," his gran said, daintily dipping her brush into a splat of blue, squeezed from a tube of 'Paints To Make Your Pictures Real', as if that was quite normal.

"You see," she laughed, as the fairy in the painting suddenly pirouetted on pointed toes, making him gasp.

"The real meadowers live all over the garden," she smiled, her green eyes creasing at the sides. His gran wore a locket that had never even opened, and every day she polished her little cream pot as if trying to make a Genie appear. It was a wonder the shamrock pattern hadn't worn off . And then she'd put the glistening pot back on a special shelf, next to the photograph of his handsome Grandpops, who the angels had taken to heaven nearly four years ago.

Ginger Nick across the street wanted to swap grans. He thought Billy's Gran was cool. "Not sure that's allowed," said Billy, thinking of Nick's toothless, haggard gran, who smelled a bit musty, and wondering what Nick would think if he knew about the fairies that were supposed to live in the garden. It was strange though, how flowers bloomed all year round, and the wind chimes jangled like a full-blown orchestra in the garden, or 'Magical Meadow' as Gran called it, but he'd never once seen a fairy. A purple heather pathway twisted through rose bushes, swaying lavender around the cherry tree, and disappeared into a patch of golden sunflowers that danced, heads bowed like ballerinas, under the moon light. "Fairy daisies," his gran told goggle-eyed neighbours who gathered every evening to gawp at the dancing flowers that glowed in the dark. At the far end of the garden, wild flowers mingled with the tall grass like paints on an artist's palette, and Billy imagined the weird meadowers spying on him. "Can you see them yet, William?" his gran asked every day. "No," he sighed, knowing that they only existed inside her head.

"Is that a fairy?" Emma asked, watching Billy's Gran swishing her paintbrush over a dainty, little figure on the canvas.

"Yes, we'll call her Emma," she said, handing her the picture of the twinkling fairy who looked just like her. Jimmy, Emma's twin, poked his nose over her shoulder, and to their surprise, the fairy in the painting jiggled her wings, showering the canvas with silver dust. His gran loved to paint, and hung pictures of mountains, forests, lakes and woodland creatures all around her cluttered house. But the Rainbow Bird was Billy's favourite. Framed in dark wood, the beautiful bird with a polished black beak and fluffy, rainbow feathers hovered between the Blueberry Mountain peaks, her turquoise eyes scanning the silvery lake below.

"Ah, I'll tell you a story about the Rainbow Bird of Glendalough if you like?" Billy's Gran said, ruffling his hair.

"The Rainbow Bird was hatched in a nest built by a blackbird, in St Kevin's outstretched hands, while he was praying," she began, and, wondering how St Kevin had stayed still for so long, the children looked at each other and frowned.

"But because she was different, the black bird deserted the little Rainbow chick, leaving St Kevin to look after her until she could fly the nest. Then, perched on his hand, he took the fully grown Rainbow Bird to the lake where, flapping her beautiful wings, she flew away."

"Ah, did he ever see her again?" Jimmy and Emma wanted to know, feeling sorry for the deserted Rainbow Bird.

"Yes. One day, a long time after, he found her hopping about the Magical Meadow with a badly broken wing."

"Ooh," said the boys, but Emma, imagining a wondrous place with twinkling lights and sparkly winged fairies in fabulous dresses, wanted to know more about the Magical Meadow.

"The Magical Meadow is by the upper lake in Glendalough, in County Wicklow, where the meadowers used to live in Ireland," Billy's Gran said, nodding towards the fairies gurning from the paintings around the garden.

"Did St Kevin bandage her wing?" Billy butted in, afraid she'd say that the meadowers lived in the garden.

"No, he carried her to a cave in the Glendalough hills where he bathed her broken wing in the water of a healing well," she said, lowering her voice.

"A healing well," they repeated, swinging their legs on the garden bench, their eyes wide.

"Yes, and as soon as the gentle water touched it, she was flapping her wing wildly again. And, gratefully pecking Saint Kevin on the cheek, she soared into the Glendalough Mountains and disappeared into the Wicklow sky," Billy's Gran finished, fluttering her fingers like little wings.

"That's a lovely story," Emma sighed, picturing the Rainbow Bird's beautiful wings carrying her over the Magical Meadow and into the purple mountains.

"What about the healing well?" Billy asked, dodging his gran's hand that was about to slap down his sticky-up hair.

"If you ever go to Ireland, you can visit the ruins of the monastic village of St Kevin of Glendalough, as he's better known these days. There's a church and a tower, and his bed, which is really just a slab, is visible above the upper lake too. There's even a well. But the whereabouts of the healing well in the cave is long forgotten," she said.

"What happened to the Rainbow Bird?" Jimmy asked, gazing into the sky as if expecting to see her.

"She's magical," Emma said, as the fairy in the painting fluttered her twinkly wings again, making her jump.

"The Rainbow Bird still hovers over the Wicklow Mountains," his gran said.

"Why doesn't she know where the well is then?" Billy laughed.

"The caves all look the same, so you see, it could be anywhere," his gran smiled. The twins turned their blonde heads and looked through the window at the painting, their eyebrows knitting as the Rainbow Bird winked a turquoise eye.

"How do you know, Gran?" Billy asked, his eyes like green pools as he studied her face.

"She told me, silly," she whispered.

Chapter 2

The Ferry

Flouncing out of the house, Billy slammed the door and sat on the wall. His gran couldn't be that crazy, she still wouldn't let him ride his bike to the park.

"Throw us the ball, Billy," said Nick, his wild, ginger curls springing as he bounced across the road on the balls of his feet. Not in the mood for Nick and his unruly hair, Billy snatched up the little, red ball.

"What's up mate, can't ride yer bike to the park?" Jimmy asked, his brakes squealing as he stopped abruptly outside Billy's Gran's.

"She might change her mind, it's only the shhhecond week of the holidays," Emma said, her teeth gummed up with toffee. Then, steadying her girly pink bike, she offered Billy a sweet from a tatty paper bag.

"She won't," Billy said, refusing the sweet and lobbing the ball to Nick, who leapt up and caught it quickly, nearly leaving his ginger curls behind. "Sure now, haven't I enough worries without ye gallivanting with them twinnies?" Wagging his finger, Jimmy mimicked his gran's Irish accent and laughing at his friend Billy, jumped on his bike and took off.

"Where yah going?" Jimmy called.

"Nowhere much," said Billy, his voice fading as he peddled like crazy down the street,

"Your gran will go schnuts," Emma warned, still chewing toffee.

Streaks of silver, black, red and pink flashed over wasteland, the twin's bikes churning up dust clouds as they chased after Billy. Zipping down bumpy alleyways, through parks and narrow streets until finally, flushed and rosy cheeked, they caught up with him outside the port.

"Where's it going?" Jimmy panted, resting his feet on the ground in the shadow of a huge ferry.

"Ireland," Billy said, pointing out the 'Irish Ferries' sign on its funnel. The water gently lapped against the ferry's sides. Swirling, squawking seagulls dived for food, and, dwarfed by the ferry, the fishing boats bobbed around it like toys in a bath. As they watched the cars and lorries driving deep into its belly, they wondered if Ireland was full of fairies, like in Billy's Gran's paintings.

"Oi! You lot, stop right there!" They heard someone yelling above the ferry's blasting funnel. Turning around, they saw Mr. Nimrev – his black, beady eyes glaring as he scuttled through the traffic like a rat. "Billy Kane, come back here, you little brat," he snarled, his face puce. Billy could picture him, watching Gran from behind his twitching net curtains. 'I bet he couldn't wait to jump in his car,' he thought. Doing an about turn, they zoomed in the opposite direction. Even Gran, who liked everybody couldn't stand him. He reminded her of someone very nasty, but she wouldn't say who.

"That feller wants to know everybody's business," she said one day, when he'd asked loads of questions about Billy. "How long was he staying? Where in London did he live again? Why was he staying with his gran?" Blah, blah, blah. A squeal of brakes pierced the air and hoping a no. 7 Bus had sent "Ratty" flying into orbit, they turned around. But no such luck. Having survived a near collision with a taxi, his fat frame was lumbering back to his abandoned car. One by one, they reached the other side of the road, bumped their bikes over the kerb and vanished into the mouth of an alleyway. Ratty's battered green Volkswagen screeched past the entrance, and catching a glimpse of their silver wheels, it squealed into reverse. Seeing his loathsome face staring down the alley, they zoomed to the bottom, with the smell of burning rubber wafting in their nostrils.

"We're lost, aren't we?" Emma wheezed, gawping at the higgledy-piggledy houses and bungalows around the strange cul-de-sac.

"Nah, we'll find our way home. I'd rather face Gran than rat man," Billy said. But there was no escaping him and, spotting the three fugitives, Ratty roared into the cul-de-sac, screeched to a halt, squeezed through the car door, and stood towering over them.

"Your grandmother's worried sick," he bellowed, foam oozing from the corners of his mouth like a rabid rat. They wondered if he had a rat's tail, and if it was a coincidence that his name spelled vermin backwards. He circled Billy, smirking and stroking his wiry moustache then, grabbing him by the scruff of the neck, he threw him into the back seat.

"You'll not be seeing these two for a while," he snapped, slamming the car door shut. Frozen with fear, Jimmy and Emma watched as he fastened Billy's bike to the roof rack. Then dabbing his forehead with a giant hanky, pulled from his too-tight jacket, he squeezed into the driver's seat, crunched the car into gear and sped off with his captive. Emma's eyes welled up seeing Billy's face squashed against the car window.

"Don't cry, Em, it was Billy's idea to do a runner," Jimmy said. As the car disappeared around the corner, Jimmy squashed his nose with his finger and Emma burst out laughing.

Wagging her finger, Billy's Gran peered over her half-moon spectacles like an owl. "You could've been killed, the port is over a busy main road," she snapped, horrified he'd cycled so far.

"But Ratty Nimrev was going to kill us," Billy said, looking for sympathy.

"If it hadn't been for Mister Nimrev, goodness knows where you'd have got to," she snapped, offering no sympathy at all.

"But, Gran," Billy whispered, hands spread in surprise. "You should've seen his face, it was as purple as a grape and very scary."

Trying not to laugh, Gran croaked, "You'll stay in the garden from now on."

"But I can't ride my bike or play football in the garden," Billy whined, shocked at the terrible punishment.

"Well, you should have thought about that before gallivanting with them twinnies," she snapped, and Billy couldn't help smirking. "We'll have picnics in the park, it'll keep you out of trouble," she said more gently, as he closed his bedroom door.

Exhausted, Billy lay on his bed and fell into a deep sleep. In his dream, he was on the ferry, bouncing across the Irish Sea and above it, a beautiful Rainbow Bird was swooping in and out of the fluffy clouds. He woke up with a start and, sitting up cross-legged, he stared at the dated Spiderman wallpaper and let his salty tears roll down his cheeks. He missed his mum, he didn't even know why she was in hospital.

"Don't worry your little head, pet," Gran said whenever he asked. He hadn't seen his dad, who lived in America with his new wife, since last Christmas and now, his crazy gran was planning picnics in the park! These summer holidays were the pits! Remembering his dream, Billy had an idea: why not run away to Ireland? If he found the healing well in Glendalough, he could cure his mum with the healing water just like St Kevin had cured the Rainbow Bird. Ratty said that stowing away on a Ferry was 'a piece of cake', so what if he was trying to get rid of him? It was a brilliant idea.

Sat on her squashy armchair, Gran was sewing little pearl buttons on a frothy, white princess dress.

"Sorry, Gran," he whispered, kissing her cheek and avoiding her eyes in case she read his mind.

A smile dimpled her cheeks as she looked up. "When you're older, you'll see that I was right. Now, I've kept you some tea," she said, squeezing his hand.

"No thanks, Gran, I'm not hungry, I just want a drink," he said. Craftily snatching crisps, biscuits and a bottle of water from the kitchen, he bounded upstairs, stuffed them in a rucksack and climbed into bed fully clothed. When the clock on the landing chimed two, Billy slipped from his bed and put on his shoes and jacket in the dark.

"I promise to find the well, Gran," he whispered blowing her a kiss outside her bedroom door. Downstairs, he quickly scribbled a note, then spying Gran's little pot on the hallway table, he stuffed it in his rucksack and clicked the front door shut.

Billy ran all the way to the port, his trainers thudding softly on the pavement with the Bond theme playing in his head. Dum di-di dum dum dum – dum di-di dum dum dum – der der – der, dah, der. James Bond was his favourite and even though he was nearly nine his gran said he was 'far too young for that rubbish'. His dad didn't mind though, as long as he looked away from any rude or gory bits. He stopped, and bending down, hands on his knees to catch his breath, he eyed the twinkling lights of the port. It was as silent as a graveyard, except for the water lapping against the quayside. And ducking under the barrier, Billy Bond 007 galloped across the tarmac and up the ferry ramp on yet another dangerous mission. A light flashed across the deck, blinding him for a second, and, ducking, he rolled behind a thick, steel girder. The light moved away and he peeped out at the two enemy agents, jackets glowing, as they flicked torches around the deck. Taking a deep breath, Bond clasped his hands together and pointed his fingers forward then, jerking the imaginary gun from side to side, he flew up two flights of stairs and disappeared into a dark recess.

Voices were coming from above and even worse, there were footsteps thudding down the stairs. In a complete panic, Bond rattled the door handle frantically. The door gave way, he tumbled inside and fired, peeow, peeow, peeow, and with the Bond theme still playing in his head, he blew down the barrel and kicked the door shut. His pulse was racing and lying on the hard, wooden floor he stared up at the ugly, chugging, hissing pipes that snaked across the walls and the ceiling. This running away lark was far too scary; maybe if he'd asked nicely, Gran would've taken him to Ireland. Pulling his blue-hooded jacket up around his ears to shut out the deafening noise, he closed his eyes and prayed that the voices would soon go away.

Chapter 3

Patsy

Disappointed that Ireland was grey, and not emerald green and purple like his gran's paintings, Billy turned from the porthole and stepped over the sick patch. Rummaging in his rucksack for some crisps, he came across the little pot, which he'd forgotten all about. His gran opened it easily enough, he thought guiltily, twisting the stubborn lid, which was harder than he thought. Then, carefully tucking the little pot between his knees, he pulled the lid until beads of sweat stood out on his forehead and his eyeballs were bulging. There was definitely something inside, he thought, holding it up to the light, and wrapping it in his jacket, tongue clenched between his teeth he heaved until he was blue in the face. Just as the lid began to loosen, the pot slipped from his grasp, bounced on the floor and smashed into smithereens.

Colourful sparks exploded in Billy's face and he ducked as dozens of stars spun out of control, whistling, crackling, fizzing and whirring around his head. "Shushhhhhh, please," he hissed, scrambling on his hands and knees, trying to gather the broken pieces together as, whirling like Catherine wheels, the stars filled the room with colourful smoke and made a terrible din. A green flash dashed through his legs and he jumped up,

"Ya *eejit,* what do ye think ye are playing at?" a cranky voice spat from behind.

"Who, who's that?" stammered Billy, turning and waving the smoke from his eyes.

"Ye nearly killed me," the voice snarled.

"It was an accident," Billy croaked, wondering where on earth the voice was coming from.

The smoke cleared and Billy gasped at the tiny, grey bearded man standing on the ledge, scrutinising him with his piercing blue eyes. Barely three inches tall, he wore an emerald green suit, a matching hat, shiny black boots and a black, leather belt pulled tightly around his generous middle.

"Look at the state of me suit!" he snapped, frantically brushing it down.

"I'm sorry mister," Billy said, reaching out to brush down his dusty suit.

"Get off me, ye've done enough damage, what'll your gran say about her precious pot," he snarled.

Billy closed his eyes, but when he opened them again the little man was still scowling at him from the ledge.

"My gran? h h how d d do you know my gran? Were you inside the little pot?" Billy stammered.

"What do you think, brains?" the little man snapped rudely.

"But what are you? Billy asked, peering into his face.

"What are ye, a moron? Ye're gran's an Irish woman and ye don't know what I am? Pah," said the little man, stepping back from Billy's inquisitive green eyes.

"No, I'm not a moron, I just can't remember what ye little people in green are called," Billy said cheekily.

"Now, if ye hadn't stolen the pot, ye wouldn't be in this mess," the leprechaun said, hopping down and stepping nimbly around the shattered pot.

"I borrowed it, that's all," Billy croaked, trying not to cry.

"Don't ye start sniveling, I'm no babysitter ye know," the little man barked.

"Good, cos I'm no baby," Billy sniffed, wiping his cheek with his sleeve. The mean little man eye-balled him for ages, his startling blue eyes never leaving his face. And just when Billy thought he was in a trance, he said:

"Okay, stop sniveling and I'll fix the pot."

"How? It's scattered into a million zillion pieces," Billy whined.

"Och, stop being so dramatic," the little man said, hopping daintily around the shards of glass. "Ye've captured me, so now I must grant ye three wishes. Which," he added, putting up one finger at a time, "are, one, not to be used to get rich, two, to harm anyone, or three, to perform some kind of miracle. Now, close your eyes before I change my mind," he barked.

"But, you're not my prisoner," Billy whispered, thinking he must be dreaming.

"Now look, ye'd better get wishing before I get fed up with ye," the little man said, snapping his eyes shut to show him how.

Billy did as he was told but, feeling daft, he opened one eye, just as the little man was scattering stuff about like nobody's business, which trickled like golden confetti and settled around the shattered pot. Then, pieces of the pot began to glide across the floor and slot into place like a jigsaw puzzle.

"Wow, there's not even a tiny crack," Billy whistled, snapping both eyes open to look at the sparkling pot.

"I'm Patsy the leprechaun," the little man said, shaking Billy's finger, which was all he could grip in his tiny hand.

"Leprechaun! That's it, now I remember! Am I really your master?" Billy asked excitedly.

"Yes, and ye have two more wishes," Patsy said begrudgingly. Boys were a pain in the neck, everyone knew that. Delighted, Billy thanked the leprechaun by patting him on the back. "Ah, let's forget that ye nearly killed me by dropping me on my head," Patsy said, beaming. Kicking up his heels, he sang, "I have a new master after all these years – his name is Billy and he's got big ears," and Billy laughed at his cheek.

The ferry docked and, grabbing the little man, Billy stuffed him in his pocket and hurried down the stairs. And attaching himself to a family of mum, dad, three kids and a granddad, he crept off the ferry unnoticed.

"Phew, that was close. Couldn't you have magicked me off or something?" Billy asked, plonking the rumpled leprechaun on the grass.

"Ye've already wasted a wish fixing a pot and now ye want to fritter another. Wish yeself home before ye get into real trouble," Patsy barked, thumping his battered hat back into shape.

"But I have to find the healing well to cure my mum," Billy said, confused by the leprechaun's mood.

"And what about ye're poor gran? She'll be climbing the walls worrying while ye're looking for a healing well that is merely a fairy tale."

"You can talk, you're just a storybook leprechaun," Billy scoffed. Patsy turned his back on Billy and tapped his foot angrily.

"I left a note for Gran," Billy whispered, regretting what he'd said, but Patsy just carried on tapping. "Fine, go visit your family or something," Billy said, trying to get rid of him.

"I've no family, you stupid boy," he hissed.

"Well go home then, you're such a misery guts," Billy snapped, walking away.

"Hey, hang on, Billy boy, not so fast. I'm sticking to ye like glue, if only for ye're gran's sake," Patsy said, hurrying after him.

"What are you doing now?" Billy asked, irritated by Patsy who, with every few yards, thrust a stick into the hedgerow like a sword.

"If ye must know, I'm looking for the curly road. It's a short cut to the Magical Meadow," he said, stabbing the hedgerow again.

"But they're not real, they're just places in Gran's stories, aren't they?"

"Ah, here it is at last. Are ye coming, or are ye just going to stand gassing all day?" Patsy asked, crawling into a gap in the hedge.

"Just answer me for once," Billy pleaded with the soles of the Leprechaun's disappearing boots.

"Yes, yes, of course they're real places. But what do I know, I'm just a story book *leprechaun*," he said, his blue eyes blinking from the other side of the gap.

Billy looked around, not sure what to do. Then lying on his belly, he wriggled after him.

"Wow! This is more like Gran's Ireland," he said, standing up to look at the green hills and the purple mountains.

"Welcome to Glendalough," said Patsy, and, feeling like he was getting somewhere at last, Billy spun several perfect cartwheels, making the leprechaun dizzy.

"Will ye quit larking about or we'll be in trouble," an irritable Patsy barked.

"Eh, what kind of trouble?" Billy asked, surprised by his pasty face.

"Oh, for pity's sake, just get a move on," Patsy snapped, following the heather covered road that wound through the hills like purple ribbon.

Dear Gran,
I'm sorry, I had to go to Ireland. Please don't worry about me.
If I find the well, I'll bring home some healing water for Mum.
Be back soon,
Luv you lots,
Billy xxx

P.S. I took the little pot to remind me of you x

Running her hand frantically along the shelf, Billy's Gran read his crumpled note. The pot was gone. Going into the garden, she shakily put her fingers either side of her mouth and gave a loud, shrill whistle.

"William's run away to Ireland and he's taken the pot," she cried, as if talking to an invisible person.

A light breeze rustled the leaves on the trees, lifting the folds of her dress and gently blowing her grey, blonde hair around her shoulders. Then, whooshing around the garden, it grew stronger, lifting garden tools, and whirling the furniture around like paper. The sky darkened and as the raging wind snapped branches, jangled the wind chimes ferociously and tossed the garden contents around, a terrifying cyclone hurtled around like a spinning top, and, howling like a wounded animal, it covered her from head to toe.

The wind blew itself out, exhausted, and, stepping through the leaves, Billy's Gran beckoned to the worried, little faces popping through every nook and cranny. And turning around, she watched the garden slowly moving and bursting into colour as fairies of all shapes and sizes slid down the flower stems, crawled from the flower pots and dropped from the cherry tree. Suddenly, frizzy, bearded leprechauns in emerald suits and hats, were leaping around in big hobnail boots, as pretty wispy-winged fairies, in raggedly hemmed dresses, flitted from flower to flower. Next, weasel-faced fairies with pointed ears, wearing shoes with curled-up toes, appeared, then folks with tufty sideburns, mending shoes with shiny hammers, and chubby folk with orange hair. Then came peculiar, bug-eyed fairies with spindly legs and buzzing, blue wings, and, lastly, dainty, transparent fairies with haunted eyes that fluttered around the garden like tiny, little ghosts. Hardly able to believe their ears, the chattering meadowers gathered around her feet, and then, looking up, they gasped to see her tears.

"Please, you mustn't go, it's far too dangerous," a marmalade-haired creature spoke out, the tears spilling from her violet eyes.

"But I must bring him home," Billy's Gran said, stooping to mop the fairy's tears with her tissue.

"But the Merrow said…"

"Never mind what the Merrow said, William is my grandson," she interrupted before the fairy finished.

Chapter 4

Princess Erin and the Meadowers,

A long time ago

With her papery wings silhouetted by the morning sun, Princess Erin fluttered over the Palace's jagged turrets. The pretty, pink buds, sprouting from the twisted, grey brambles, made it look much less like a haunted castle. Drifting downwards, the breeze blowing her flaxen blonde hair, and her green eyes glinting, she landed softly by the rippling upper lake. Then, guiltily looking around, she put her fingers in her mouth and gave two, short, sharp toots.

"Must you, Erin, it's not fairy like, is it?" her father, King Marty, would tut whenever he caught her whistling. While her mother, Queen Olivia would say, "a whistling meadow fairy and a crowing hen, never came to no good end," whatever that meant. Today though, it seemed like she'd got away with it.

The leaves shivered, the grass swayed, and frizzy-bearded leprechauns, muddy marsh fairies, pointy-eared pixies and folk with bushy sideburns, who were mending shoes with shiny hammers, popped out of the quivering bushes. Curtains of the long violet grass parted and out stepped gnomes with knobbly feet, elves in stripy outfits, chubby folk with violet eyes and marmalade hair, and meadow fairies in sparkling ballerina gowns, who twirled dizzily around her. Then bug eyed fairies, with peacock blue wings, and ghostly fairies in billowing

31

gowns, came drifting from the trees. Clapping, the Princess spun around, giggling at the fluttering halo around her head.

"Let's take the water chariot out on the lake," she cried above the excited chatter, and removing their tiny shoes, the meadowers helped her to push the heavy, oak water chariot onto the lake with a splash.

On board the chariot, the Princess cracked her slim, sparkly wand, and a fuzzy storm cloud appeared, like a scribbling in the clear blue sky. Seeing the fearful eyes looking up, Windy Wendy puffed out her cheeks and blew, sending the chariot hurtling across the lake. As huge silvery waves crashed over the chariot's deck, water gushed through its leaky bottom.

"Too much, Wendy," the Princess called, over the screeching of the meadowers, but enjoying it far too much, the angry storm cloud blew harder. Shredded by the howling wind, the chariot's flower petal sails whirled like confetti, and the winged fairies fled over the lake like a swarm of mosquitoes. Alarmed by the leprechauns, gnomes and pixies leaping overboard, the Princess fluttered her saturated wings and, swishing her wand, she called, *"Magic wand I fear – the damage will be worse if Windy Wendy doesn't disappear,"* and with a bright flash, the cloud was gone.

Most afternoons, the mischievous meadowers had lots of fun with the people walking in the Blueberry, Glendalough hills.

"How did you get here so fast?" The Princess asked, eyeing the traffic jam stretching down the lane, caused by the leprechaun's favourite trick of switching the road signs around.

"A sprinkling of fairy dust on our boots and we're leaping like frogs," Patsy sniggered. The Princess, though, wasn't looking forward to another afternoon of tickling faces with papery wings and whispering in ears like a naughty ghost.

"Sure, there's no point in being invisible if ye can't mess with the beans," Patsy said cheekily, glad to be invisible to the angry drivers tooting and swearing around him.

"Be-**ings**," the Princess laughed, although disappointed, that she still hadn't met a single *bean, (as Patsy called them)* with the gift of sight to talk to about something other than stupid, fairy dust.

The Princess liked catching the long, green, fire-breathing shingle dragons that lived on the shore. First, she'd chase the shingle dragon which had orange bumps to the tip of its tail, and could scamper on little feet or slither on its belly, until yellow flames were flicking from its flared nostrils. Then, grabbing it by the tail, she'd whirl it around her head and let it fly across the lake where, landing with a splash, it would sizzle like a red-hot poker, and make spectacular, orange steam clouds that hovered over the water. And then, with the bright orange puffs trailing behind it, the confused shingle dragon would snake, lazily, back to shore.

When not teasing the beans or hurling flame-breathing shingle dragons into the lake, the artistic Princess sat quietly in the Magical Meadow stitching hems, sewing on buttons and sketching the wildlife that drank from the babbling brook. Soon, drifting like dandelion seeds and seeping from secret corners, the meadowers came to listen to one of her many stories.

"What story would you like?" the Princess asked the cross-legged, nattering, semi-circle gathering around her.

"The Banshees!"

"The Sea Malion!"

"The Sea Merrow!"

Numerous voices called out numerous requests, their hands waving impatiently.

"What about the 'Stranger's Story'?" the Princess whispered secretively.

"Who's he?" snapped a rubbery faced elf with his heart set on the 'Sea Malion', which was a human headed seal monster, that swallowed whole ships.

"The Stranger saved the Magical Meadow a long time ago, by driving out the rat boys and the pooka (hobgoblins)," said the Princess. The disgruntled elf shrugged. "Never heard of him," he said, sitting down and crossing his big, knobbly feet.

"A long time ago," the Princess began, *"Tia, the tree spirit, saw the Stranger, riding a winged, grey horse through the meadow. Behind him, a band of hobbling winged imps hacked at the undergrowth. Dressed smartly, he wore a snow-white shirt and black breeches, with a sinister black hood covering his face. Staring through the eye slits, his cool blue eyes sought out Tia, who was hidden in the brambles. 'Don't be afraid, tree spirit, someone has asked for my help,' he boomed."*

"What was he looking for?" barked the irritable elf, picturing the hooded stranger and his horse, its wings swishing slowly as it trotted through the meadow.

"Well..." *she continued. "Gently flicking the horse's reins, he led the imps into the muddy marshes, and, finding the sleeping rat boys in their nests, they tipped their hairy torsos into the lake with a plop."*

The little meadowers gasped at their bravery. "So that's why we don't have to live under the ground anymore," said Charlotte, the marsh fairy, smoothing her raggedy, hemmed dress.

"Yes, it was the Stranger who freed us from the rat boys," the Princess smiled.

"Then, unfolding their raggedy wings," she went on, *"the imps swooped around the meadow, chasing away the pooka,*

who, *petrified for their lives, hauled themselves so quickly over the rocks that they ripped out their fingernails, leaving a trail of blood behind. Then, long tails snaking behind them, a huddle of rat boys slithered through the marshes to sink their sharp fangs into the shins of the beautiful horse.*" She lowered her voice and then, playfully snapping her teeth, she made them jump before going on.

"*And, eyes bulging, the Stranger swished his sword through the muddy water and chopped off their heads.*"

"Ooooooooooh" the meadowers gasped again, their hands clamped over their mouths.

"'*Swim you idiots!' Finbar, their chief, boomed as he led the floundering rat boys, through the murky water, with the flying imps' arrows raining from above. Spying Finbar's whiskers skimming the water, the Stranger whipped his horse into a gallop and chased after him. But, knowing the lake and its secrets, the sly rat boy slipped under the water and disappeared.*"

"Oh no!" they cried, disappointed for the brave Stranger.

"'*The meadow belongs to King Marty and the meadowers, I'll return should Finbar ever come back,' the Stranger told Tia, who'd finally come out of hiding. Then, galloping into the distance, his fine horse flapping its leathery wings, he soared into the Wicklow sky and disappeared, along with the band of raggedy-winged imps.*"

"Who asked for his help?" a chubby meadower asked, his wide, violet eyes staring from under his thick, orange fringe.

"That must remain a secret," the Princess whispered.

Chapter 5

Finbar and the rat boys

On the other side of the hedgerow, it was a beautiful bright, sunny day. In fact, it was like a different country. "Wow, it's the curly road," Billy whispered, looking at the purple road looping like a ribbon through the green fields, just like in Gran's painting.

"Quick, hide," said Patsy, suddenly leaping into the long grass and leaving him standing alone.

"What's up?" Billy asked.

"Shush," Patsy hissed, his battered hat appearing over the top of the grass. Wishing the moody leprechaun would stop frightening the life out of him, Billy leapt in beside him.

"It'll be the police looking for me," Billy whispered, hearing a scuffling noise.

"Tis not the police, get down if you want to see your granny again," Patsy snapped, his face turning the colour of pastry. Wondering if he should slap the leprechaun's face to calm him down (like in the movies), Billy ducked out of sight.

"It's the rat boys!" said Patsy, looking quite faint.

"You mean rats?" Billy gulped peering into the swaying grass.

"No, rat *boys,* they run on two legs as well as four, and have beady eyes, snouts, whiskers, and long, black tails to whip you senseless. And they carry a shillelagh to knock your block off. What do you think of that, Billy boy?" Patsy asked, almost out of breath.

"They carry what to knock your block off?" Billy asked, not sure what to make of any of it.

"A shill-lay-lee, a knobbly piece of wood carved from a blackthorn tree. If ye get a thump from a shillelagh ye'll know all about it," Patsy said.

"But they're just fairies, I'll stamp on them if they come near us," said Billy, pulling himself up to his full height.

"No, no, they're cunning," Patsy said, dramatically shielding his eyes to look up and down the lane.

"Gran says people who see fairies are special," Billy said, changing the subject.

"Ye, Billy boy, have no idea how special ye are," Patsy quipped, leaving him more confused than ever.

"I know, how about ye wish yeself home?" Patsy suggested after a moments silence.

"Are you still mad because I broke the pot?" Billy asked suspiciously.

"Nope, it's just too dangerous for a little fella like yeself," Patsy tutted.

"Can I use the wish to find the well?" Billy asked.

"Nope, it's been tried before," Patsy said shaking his head.

"Okay, the wishes are useless anyway, and I suppose Gran could come back to Ireland to help me to find the well," Billy shrugged, secretly not liking the sound of the rat boys anyway.

"So ye'll do it then?" asked Patsy, relieved, and yet annoyed to hear his wishes were useless. "Great, now close ye're eyes, I'll blast ye, and ye'll be back in good auld blighty in no time," he said. Opening a leather pouch, he scattered the dust and gabbled, "*Golden dust scattered on the land – hurry to take Billy safely home to his gran,*" and shutting his eyes, Billy prayed she wouldn't be too mad.

Billy's head spun until he was dizzy and then, spinning out of control, he corkscrewed into the ground and disappeared. That wasn't supposed to happen. Usually the 'wisher' was swallowed by a flattering, softer light, Patsy thought, examining the smouldering patch on the grass. "Wait for the spinning to stop, ye might feel dizzy and sick, ye've never been dusted before," he called down the hole, not sure if Billy could hear him.

Turning head over heels, Billy bumped his head so many times he thought it was going to fall off. Just when he thought he would never stop, he landed at the bottom with a thud.

"Gran, I'm back," he called, spitting out spiders and worms and flicking creepy crawlies from his face.

"Useless," he muttered, listening to his echo eerily calling for his Gran in the dark, musty cave.

A blast of hot breath on the back of his neck made him spin around, to find a huge, hairy figure looming in the dark, its long, black tail sweeping the ground as it moved.

"Well, well, a boy," it rasped, and swishing its crimson cloak, it studied Billy's face with its black, beady eyes. The huge, ugly rat sniffed Billy's clothes, its wiry whiskers brushing his cheek and making him stumble backwards with fright.

"You're huge," Billy croaked, recognising the rat boy from Patsy's description. It even had a thingamajig in its claw to bash his brains in.

"The leprechaun isn't the only one who can do magic tricks," the fearsome rat boy rasped, showing its sharp teeth. Billy gulped, and then he saw an embarrassed Patsy, who looked much larger too, staring through the bars of a cage. Everything was huge, the rocks were as big as mountains, the flickering flame was miles above him, and the trickling water was thundering in his ears. Oh no, his stomach flipped, the Irish Rat had shrunk him and now, as Gran would say, 'he was no bigger than two tall hats.'

"Well, numbskull, you worked out that *a boy with the gift of sight* could set you free from the pot," the rat boy laughed at Patsy, his foul breath polluting the air.

"Come on, Patsy, use your gold dust, it might work," Billy called, worried the leprechaun was in a trance. Dangling Patsy's precious pouch of gold dust, the rat boy grabbed Billy, and, opening the cage door, he threw him in too.

A smaller rat boy scuttled from the dark, and fastening the rope on the cage door in a big fat knot, it squashed its ugly face against the bars and growled. "Don't you recognise me, Billy?"

As its fur began to drop off and smoke poured from its ears, Billy was shocked to see that it wasn't a rat boy, it was Mr. Nimrev, Gran's nosy neighbour.

"Wha, wha, what happened?" Billy stammered.

"Shame about the healing well, what a touching story that would've made," Mr. Nimrev rasped, and, twirling his wiry whiskers, he swished his grey cloak and turned into a rat boy again, as if Billy had imagined the whole thing.

"It'll be worth it when she follows you," the bigger rat boy snarled, and with long black tails sweeping the floor, they scurried into the darkness.

"Well, look, ye're like a wee leprechaun," Patsy joked.

"It's not funny, wait till Gran sees the state of me," Billy snapped, glaring into Patsy's blue eyes, now level with his own.

"I was right about ratty Nimrev. Did you see his tail? He is a rat! But what's he doing in Glendalough, and who's going to follow me?" Billy asked, glad they'd gone.

"I don't have a clue what they're blathering on about," Patsy shrugged.

"Are there just two rat boys in the cave?" Billy asked, peering into the darkness.

"Nope, more like two or three hundred," Patsy said.

"What! Are you joking?" Billy shuddered, thinking of all those wriggling tails and twitching whiskers.

"Nope, so while they're having a kip, we'd better find a way out," Patsy said.

"What did the bigger rat boy mean by 'you needed a boy to set you free from the pot'?" Billy asked.

"Well, a long time ago, I got the Stranger to run the rat boys out of the meadow. Years later, Finbar, that's him, the chief rat boy, wedged me head first in a pot, which somehow ended up on ye're gran's shelf. If I'd known a little whipper snapper like ye could set me free, I'd have got ye to drop me on me head years ago," said Patsy.

"What, you never even thanked me!" Billy snapped, even though he wanted to laugh.

"Thank ye, what for, delivering me back to Finbar?" Patsy grumbled, rattling the cage door.

"Who is the Stranger anyway?" Billy asked sulkily.

"Ye're like a little parrot, ye never stop squawking. I don't know, he wore a black hood."

Tutting, Billy lay on his belly to reach a piece of flint, just as a winged shadow flew over the cage, blocking out the light.

"Wow, I don't believe it, it's the Rainbow Bird," Billy squealed.

Sure enough, perched on the rocks above, the dazzling bird from Gran's painting was watching them with her turquoise eyes. Spreading out her multicoloured wings, she circled the cage, swooped down, scooped up the flint in her shiny, black beak and dropped it through the bars.

All afternoon they sawed at the thick rope until, with his hands tired and blistered, Billy lobbed the flint on the ground.

"Well, that's a great help," Patsy said sarcastically.

"It's no good, it's never going to work," Billy moaned. Picking up the flint, Patsy hacked the rope again, until the door of the cage swung open.

"High five, wimp," he said slapping his hand against Billy's as they stumbled into darkness. The cave was mucky and, squelching through the puddles, they ducked under some jagged spikes that met in the middle like giant dinosaur's teeth. Then, tiptoeing past the straw nests of snoring rat boys, they hauled each other upwards over the rock face, and, hearts hammering, they looked up at the inviting blue sky peeping teasingly through the roof.

"One more tricky bit, and we'll be home and dry," Patsy panted, reaching out for Billy's hand. But, losing his footing, Billy wobbled and tumbled painfully downwards, knocking himself out on a rock with a sickening thud. Patsy scrambled to the edge and looked down. Billy's face was ghostly white and, seeing blood trickling from a cut above his eye, he began to wail. Opening his eyes, Billy squinted up at the blurry leprechaun, who was making the most dreadful noise, and rolling over, he snuggled back into the warm carpet.

"Don't panic, Billy boy, I'm coming to get ye," the leprechaun said. A loud purrrrrrrrrrrrrrrr vibrated underneath Billy and, sitting bolt upright, he found himself staring into a pair of hard, black eyes. Jumping up quickly, he leapt onto the wall.

"Patsy, help, I've landed on a big fat rat!" he yelled. Annoyed, the rat boy grabbed his ankle, yanking him towards its wide-open jaws. Feeling its needle-sharp teeth pricking his skin, Billy dug his fingernails into the wet earth and closed his eyes. A loud THWACK rang in his ear and, suddenly free from the rat boy's grasp, he turned to find Patsy, shillelagh (shill-lay-lee) in hand, dancing a jig on top of the unconscious rodent.

"Told ye ye'd feel it, if ye got a thump from one of these," he beamed.

"Patsy, you're a legend!" Billy cried, throwing his arms around the leprechaun's neck.

Claws scratched over the rocky surface as a mass of rat boys suddenly swept through the cave, moving like a black carpet. If ever Patsy needed his magic dust, it was right now. Loose rocks tumbled under their feet as they scrambled higher, trying to escape the nightmare of wriggling tails and twitching whiskers scampering after them.

"Look, Patsy, she's back," Billy squealed, ducking as the Rainbow Bird, her wings flapping furiously, skimmed their heads and swept the scampering Rat boys from the rocks.

"STRIKE!" yelled Patsy, leaping up and punching the air as tangled fur balls, tails and shillelaghs (shill-lay-lees) tumbled downwards.

"Look, she's waiting for us!" Billy screamed, grabbing Patsy's hand to drag him over the rocks to clamber onto her downy back. With them gratefully clinging onto her rainbow feathers, the Rainbow Bird flapped her magnificent wings, and, soaring upwards, she sailed through the gap and out into the blue Wicklow sky.

Billy wanted to laugh, surely he was dreaming? The Rainbow Bird, from his gran's painting, had rescued him and his leprechaun friend from the Rat boys? He closed his eyes, as she crashed through a poodle-shaped cloud. Then opening them again, he gawped at her wings, whooshing up and down like rainbow fans. His hair was damp, and his cheeks were burning from the biting wind as they flew over silvery waterfalls, purple mountains, people, no bigger than ants, and emerald green farmland, dotted with miniature animals like a farm set he'd had when he was little. The Rainbow Bird dive-bombed downwards and, cheeks rattling, Billy clutched her feathers as she glided over the green canopy of the forest. Then fluttering on to the twisted branch of an old, oak tree she neatly folded her wings. Billy looked over his shoulder – poor Patsy's face was as green as his suit, "Oh, I was never a good flyer," he said.

"Where are we now?" Billy asked, hardly giving him time to recover.

"We're still in Glendalough, and this fine tree is home to the tree spirits. Ye never know, they might help us to find the well," he said, spitting out rainbow feathers. Then, sliding off the Rainbow Bird's broad back, he firmly placed his boots on the knobbly branches.

Chapter 6

Shane

A long time ago

Mcloughlin's farm was a peaceful haven after the shenanigans of the meadow. And, except for Billy the goat, who went berserk, butting the fence with his stubby horns, the animals were always pleased to see the Princess.

"That goat's a menace, you never know what mood he'll be in," Mr. McLoughlin, the farmer, complained to his wife.

"Maybe it's because he can see the fairies dancing, like our Shane used to," Mrs. Mcloughlin laughed, as the angry goat chased the farmer around the pen, unaware that, across the yard, a mischievous Princess Erin was pulling faces and making the goat ten times worse. Every day, Mrs. McLoughlin, a round woman with a kind face and twinkling blue eyes, piled her steel grey hair into an untidy bun to bake soda bread, cakes, loaves and tarts. Her equally round husband, his face red from harsh winds and his eyes bloodshot from too much whiskey, would ride Neddy, the ginger carthorse, around the hilly farm, and with Tess, the black and white collie dog, he'd check on the chestnut cows, the yellow-eyed sheep, and the scatterings of chickens, geese and ducks.

The Princess's favourite place was the cosy farmhouse kitchen. While she was sampling a delicious, fresh batch of baking, she heard Mrs. Mcloughlin screaming from the yard. And, barely able to fly after eating so much, she darted outside to see thick, black, smoke billowing from underneath the barn door. Heart hammering, she zipped underneath the door to find vicious, yellow flames licking around the farmer's legs, and his wife trying to put out the flames with a pitcher of water.

The Princess flicked her wand. *"Bucket quick, make haste – fill with water – there's no time to waste,"* she spluttered, her eyes smarting from the smoke.

An electric blue flash zig zagged across the barn, lifting a bucket from the door. Then, floating to the raging flames, it poured endless water, putting the fire out and sending blue smoke swirling around the barn.

"Did you see that? The bucket with a hole in it put out the fire," the blackened farmer coughed.

"Floating buckets, whatever next, pink elephants? 'Twas me who put out the fire, you stupid man," Mrs. Mcloughlin lied, while blessing herself.

"What?! No more drinking for me, I'm seeing things, I am," the shocked farmer spluttered, as his wife patted his back. Coughing, the farmer picked his way over the blackened hay and, giggling, the Princess tucked her wand away.

Shane Mcloughlin, their son, came home for good later that week. His grandmother had sadly passed away and now he was no longer needed to run the farm. Tall, with wavy chestnut hair and blue eyes, the Princess thought he was very good-looking.

"Eat up son, there is apple pie afterwards," his proud Ma said, staggering under a bubbling pot of Irish stew, made especially for his homecoming dinner. Shane rubbed his big hands together, as he took a deep sniff of the stew. Suddenly dropping the saltcellar with a clang, he jumped up.

"Ahhhhhhhhhhhh," he cried, as if he'd seen a ghost.

"A mou, a mou, a mouse," he stammered. Wasting no time, Ma bashed the table with a rolling pin.

"And you, a big strapping farmer," Da roared, but the Princess, already devouring the dumpling crumbs, hadn't seen a thing.

"Will you have a drop of ale, Da?" Shane asked, pouring himself a long, frothy drink from a jug.

"No thanks, son, I don't touch it anymore," he said.

"What? Are you sick, Da?" Shane asked, surprised.

"No, he gave up drinking when he dropped his pipe on the hay, set fire to the barn, and swore a floating bucket with a hole in it had tipped water over the fire until it had gone out," Ma said.

"When did this happen?" asked Shane, putting his drink down.

"Just two weeks ago," Ma laughed uneasily.

"Was it a big fire?" Shane asked, concerned.

"Ay, big enough," Da nodded, taking a puff of his pipe.

"Who put it out then?"

"Me of course," said Ma, her face turning bright crimson as she wiped her hands on her apron.

"And, how did you put it out, Ma?" Shane asked.

"Er, er, with a pitcher of water," she stammered.

"My dearest, you saved my life, but I can only give you what has been in my family for years," said Da, handing her a package. Grateful to him for distracting Shane, Ma opened the package to find a shiny, gold, oval locket and a tiny, cream pot which had three hand-painted shamrocks on the front.

"The lid of the pot is a bit stiff, and the locket has never opened, but there's space on the back for an engraving," Da said, enjoying being in the good books for a change.

"You're better off without the drink," Ma said, pleased with the gifts, and still watching Shane from the corner of her eye.

Shane was baffled. Ma couldn't have put the fire out with a pitcher of water, there was too much damage. Feeling exhausted after hours of clearing the blackened hay, and measuring, sawing and fitting new panels he sat down to eat. The Princess, who was hungry too, hopped onto the pocket of his red, checked shirt and waited for the crumbs to fall. Taking a bite of his sandwich at last, Shane brushed the crumbs away, making her tumble backwards.

"Ouch," she yelped, picking herself up and smoothing down her silver dress. Shane paused to look around the barn. Surely he couldn't have heard, she thought, and, as he took another bite, she fluttered upwards, and stopped directly in front of his face.

"Whoa, are you what I think you are?" asked Shane, dropping the sandwich and jumping to his feet.

"You can see me?" the Princess whispered, her wings fluttering and her green eyes twinkling.

"Yes, I saw you yesterday too. You were stealing food from the table," he prompted when Erin, still in shock, stared blankly.

"Oh, I'm sorry, your ma's such a good cook I couldn't help myself. So it wasn't a mouse then," she giggled.

"No. When I was a nipper, Ma clipped me around the ear for saying that I'd seen the fairies dancing in the fields, so I wasn't going to tell her that a meadow fairy was helping herself to her Irish stew, right under her nose," he laughed.

"My name's Erin," she whispered, trancelike, wondering what Patsy would make of her special bean.

"Well, Erin, what do you know about the mysterious fire?" Shane asked.

"Oh," she said, and flicking her wand, she lifted the bucket with an electric blue flash.

"So it was you! Ma's lying because she wants Da to stop drinking! But what does she think happened?" he asked, examining the hole in the bucket.

"Oh, she thinks it was miracle, I guess," the Princess giggled.

"Well, it was a miracle, in a way. She stopped Da drinking, didn't she?" Shane said, making her laugh again.

The Princess guided Shane around the Magical Meadow, which she shared with little fairies known as the meadowers. Fascinated by the giant, a few red-faced, cobblers, with big, bushy sideburns, hopped onto Shane's boots, and began tapping them with little hammers.

"Could you please take them off, mister? Tis very difficult," Donal, a balding cobbler, asked politely, and, though embarrassed by his tatty footwear, Shane handed them over. After they had stitched the soles and tapped the heels, the tiny cobblers polished his boots until they shone like mirrors, and, delighted, Shane put them back on.

A stony-eyed scribbling of a storm cloud huffed and puffed, blowing a water chariot across the lake. And as it cast its eyes downwards, and got ready to puff up its cheeks again, a dozen meadowers jumped into the lake.

Suddenly, a carnival of chubby, orange haired folk with amazing violet eyes came cartwheeling, juggling, and back-flipping downhill, nearly bowling Shane over.

"Hello, sir, how do you do? It's very nice to meet you – please come again soon and we can get to know you," sang the charming, rickety bridge as he crossed a babbling brook.

Squillions of bug-eyed fairies, with peacock blue wings, darted around like twinkling fireflies. Rabbits and doe-eyed deer sprang through carpets of golden daisies. Noticing the shyer meadowers watching him from the windows in the trunks of the silver-leaved trees, Shane followed Erin further into the beautiful meadow.

Near the centre of the meadow, seated on red, velvet, oversized thrones were Erin's parents, King Marty, and Queen Olivia. The fair-haired King's blue eyes twinkled, as he welcomed Shane, and then he introduced him to his dark haired Queen, who stared at him with eyes as green as Erin's. Draped in green velvet cloaks, trimmed with white fur, with gold emerald encrusted crowns sitting jauntily on their heads, Shane thought they looked every inch of the fairy tale King and Queen.

With fiddles tucked under their chins, and bows whizzing over the strings, the Leprechauns filled the meadow with feverish music. As the meadow fairies danced an Irish jig, arms arched over their heads, feet crisscrossing in perfect time, and their silvery wings glistening, the meadower's whirled each other around and around. The music ended and the amazing kaleidoscope of fairies stopped twirling. Then, shimmering in an ice blue gown, Erin sat in front of a golden harp, and letting her fingers glide expertly over the golden strings, she played a sweet and haunting melody. Shane closed his eyes to listen, and as the music drifted across the meadow and into the sky, he knew that he'd fallen in love with the fairy Princess.

Chapter 7

The Ghost Ship

"Tree spirits, who are they?" Billy asked, waving to the Rainbow Bird as she flew off into the distance.

"Friends," said Patsy, jumping from the last step and rapping on the tree trunk with a rat-a-tat-tat. A gorgeous creature with haunted eyes opened the door and hovered in the doorway; her long, tawny hair floated around her shoulders, reminding him of another of Gran's paintings.

"Patsy, come in," she said, in barely a whisper. Inside the tree, which smelled of freshly mown grass, dozens of tree spirits glided as if on roller skates around the large circular room and the warren of dark mysterious tunnels.

"Welcome to our humble home," Tia, the beautiful tree spirit, whispered, ushering them to sit on soft, squashy toadstools, where bowls of red berry stew and hot buttered corn steamed on a huge, oak table.

"How come the tree spirits keep vanishing?" Billy asked, his cheeks wriggling uncontrollably, the sudden burst of strawberry, redcurrant, raspberry and cranberry swirling around his gums as he slurped his stew. "Och, will ye stop gawping? Ye're dribbling red stuff all over ye're jacket," Patsy laughed.

"I didn't get a chance to ask the Rainbow Bird about the healing well, do you think she knows where to find it?" Billy asked Tia, dabbing his jacket with a leafy napkin.

"No, I'm sorry, it was such long time ago, even the Rainbow Bird doesn't remember. Let the rat boys forget about you, and then the ghost ship will take you across the upper lake to the caves. Although, some say that the well disappeared the day St Kevin died," she whispered, not wanting Billy to get his hopes too high. Then, noticing that he could barely keep his eyes open, she lit a lantern and showed him to a charming little bedroom along a dark tunnel. Where, climbing the wonky ladder, Billy threw himself into a soft, snowy, white hammock that wrapped around him like a cloud.

"WAKEY, WAKEY", Billy yelled in Patsy's ear, finding him hours later, snoozing in the hammock below, his little cheeks puffing in and out.

"What in the blue blazes are ye doing, it's still dark outside! What about Finbar?" Patsy barked, rubbing his ear, and guessing why Billy had woken him up.

"Tia said there's a ghost ship," Billy said, dragging the still half-asleep leprechaun to his feet.

"I didn't mean for you to go tonight, it's far too soon," and, horrified by Billy's idea, Tia faded out of sight.

"Let's see how brave ye are when the rat boys catch ye again," Patsy tutted.

"Gran will be worried," Billy said, staring at the blank wall where Tia had hovered moments before.

"Wait a couple of nights, please," she pleaded, reappearing behind him.

"But Gran will go nuts," he argued, shooing away several, stick-thin, bug-eyed creatures that were prodding him with sticks.

"Sorry, the forest guardians are just curious," she giggled. Like raindrops drumming on a tin can, as having satisfied their curiousity, they scampered away on knobbly, thin legs.

"It is a bit late to be worrying about ye're gran going nuts, isn't it?" Patsy scoffed.

"Please, Tia, my mum is very sick," Billy pleaded with her as she faded from sight again.

"Okay, okay, but the forest guardians must go too, they have special wings that will light up, in the pitch-blackness of the forest," she said, reappearing again.

"Okay, ye've got the job," Patsy laughed, shielding his eyes from the bright blue hue as, spreading their wings, the forest guardians showed them off... "Now, Billy, this is Willow, Evie, Molly and Wisp. They will whisper directions in your ears as you walk through the forest," Tia said, glancing to her right.

"Er hi," said Billy to four pairs of hazel eyes hovering beside her in thin air.

Listening carefully to the whispering tree spirits, and with the light shed from the forest guardians amazing blue wings, Billy and Patsy soon found themselves overlooking the upper lake, on the edge of the Magical Meadow. A full moon was casting a golden ribbon on the rippling black water, the leaves were rustling in the night breeze, and as an owl hooted, the outline of a ghost ship appeared on the lake. It was faint at first, and then it began to fill in, bit by bit, like a developing photograph, until at last a magnificent galleon ship was rocking on the water, her mighty sails flapping in the breeze.

"Quickly, you must leap on to the rope ladder, before she sails without you," the tree spirits whispered. And, dancing like shards of blue light, the forest guardians practically shoved them from the little stone jetty.

Patsy craned his neck, following the mast into the star spattered navy blue sky. On the lower deck, a swaying lantern cast ghostly shadows, a toppled glass dripped constantly, and a fat cigar butt smoldered, never burning out.

"Everything is the same as the day the Captain and his crew disappeared," Patsy whispered over the loud creaking and juddering of the ships joints.

"What do you think happened?" Billy croaked, wishing he'd stayed in the big, oak tree with the tree spirits.

"I doubt even the rat boys could kidnap a whole crew of cutthroats pirates," Patsy shrugged. Drifting to the far end of the lake, the ship's anchor crashed deafeningly into the water, and lowering a small boat, they scarpered down the ladder and rowed without a backward glance.

"I wish I could have another wish to get us inside the caves," Billy moaned, seeing how far they still had to go.

"Ye know that Finbar took my pouch of gold dust," Patsy snapped.

"So, when will I get my two wishes then?"

"It's no good whingeing, you said the wishes were useless anyway," Patsy scoffed. But, mesmerised by a distant glow moving downhill to the little shore, Billy ignored him.

"Are they rat boys?" Billy whispered, peeping at the shadowy figures spreading across the shore as they secured the little boat.

"Nope it's the dim wit Bally bogs," Patsy said, yanking the tail of Billy's jacket and making him duck down.

"Ooooh they're weird," Billy said, popping up again to spy on the pot-bellied, fatheaded creatures with tufts of wiry hair and gob-stopper eyes.

"They're more like aliens, except for that one," he pointed, "that kind of looks like a rat boy!" he gulped, noticing its fine whiskers under the flickering flames.

"The leprechaun and the boy were on the ghost ship – find them!" the rat-shaped silhouette barked.

"Oh no, they're still looking for us! We're never going to find the healing well," Billy said, trembling at the sight of the rat boy.

"They're not likely to have forgotten us, are they? Not when the Rainbow Bird bowled them over like skittles," Patsy hissed, annoyed that an eight-year-old boy had talked him into such a stupid plan. The flickering flames moved nearer, lighting the shore and before Patsy could stop him, Billy shot from behind the rock.

"Ruuuuunnnnn, Patsy!" he yelled, and, like a grey hound out of a trap, he dashed towards the ghost ship.

Teetering on the edge of a huge sandy drop, which, had he been a normal boy size, would have been easy to jump, Billy thought how inviting the ghost ship looked, bobbing about in the moonlight.

"Ye have to jump. Look, I'll go first," said Patsy, turning to see the bally bogs, flames flickering, bounding ever closer. And taking a leprechaun leap, he sailed over the top and landed safely in the sand. 'Quick, Billy' he urged, and, looking down, Billy jumped too, landing on a soft green mass.

"Oh no, Billy, ye've landed on a nest of flame-breathing shingle dragons!" Patsy screeched, prizing the sucker pad feet of the wriggling green and orange mass from Billy's skin with a painful pop, and hurling them into the lake. More shingle dragons, breathing scalding, yellow flames, wriggled over Billy, and breathing in Patsy's face, they set fire to his beard. Then the whole nest engulfed Billy, covering his face until he couldn't breathe.

"Talk to me, wake up, please!" Patsy pleaded into Billy's purple, lifeless face, his beard dripping from its dunking in the lake.

"I want to go home now, please," croaked Billy eventually, the colour returning to his cheeks. Relieved to hear his voice, Patsy sank his face in Billy's chest and sobbed.

The weird looking bally bogs threw them in a cell and locked the door.

"Does it hurt?" Billy asked, remembering Patsy's flaming beard as he sat on the cold damp floor.

"No, it doesn't hurt," Patsy said crossly, annoyed by the stupid smirk on Billy's face.

"William, wipe that silly grin off your face, people will think you're laughing at them," Gran always said, whenever he got the giggles, which was quite a lot.

"Thank you, Patsy, you saved my life," he said, managing to keep a straight face under the leprechaun's cold, blue stare.

"Ye should've stayed put," Patsy scoffed.

"Open up," a familiar voice rasped from outside. A key turned, and smelling worse than a wet dog and wielding a shillelagh, Finbar leapt into the cell.

"By the time I'm finished, you'll wish you'd stayed inside that cosy, little pot," he growled, pushing Patsy so hard he fell over.

"I took the pot and smashed it, that's why he's here. Please don't hurt him," Billy pleaded, helping Patsy to his feet.

"So the boy dropped you on your thick skull, you didn't work it out at all," Finbar laughed. "Now, where are King Marty and Queen Olivia?" he roared, baring his sharp black teeth, making them flinch.

"How should I know, I'm a numbskull," Patsy snapped. Finbar roared again, the stench of his breath almost knocking them out and then turning on his heel he left.

"Who are King and Queen thingy?" Billy asked, as Finbar swept out the door in a blaze of crimson.

"Never mind. When that big, fat rat comes back, I'm going to knock his block off," Patsy said, pulling a catapult from his pocket.

"Will it work?" Billy asked, admiring the catapult's gleaming, silver handle.

"Of course, why wouldn't it? I've flattened a few rat boys in my time. Now, quick, help me to find a few lethal stones," he smirked.

A sudden gust of wind blew Patsy's hat off and the tinkle of wind chimes echoed around the cell.

"There must be a storm gathering overhead," Patsy said, looking up for a gap in the roof.

"That sounded just like the wind chimes in Gran's garden," said Billy, his green eyes filling with tears.

"Och, none of that, we will be out of here in a jiffy," Patsy said gently, just as another sudden gust blew a film of silver dust around them. A strange light twinkled in the far corner of the cell, and, as they moved towards it, a familiar figure stepped through the light and into the cell.

"Gran!" Billy screamed, dropping the stones and rushing towards her.

"William!" she cried, reaching out for him as a silver cylone swirled around them. Then, with a 'Boom!' she vanished...

"What happened?" Billy cried, grabbing Patsy and shaking him. Then, with another 'Boom', a beautiful fairy appeared in her place. Wearing a silver ribbon in her flaxen blonde hair, the fairy fluttered her paper-thin wings, and smoothing her silvery dress, she batted her long, black eyelashes and fixed her familiar green eyes on Billy.

"Billy, this is Erin, the fairy Queen of the Magical Meadow," Patsy whispered, as silver dust settled around them.

Chapter 8

A new fairy queen

A long time ago

There wasn't a single bird singing in the lower meadow. With a horrible feeling in the pit of her stomach, Princess Erin floated down to look closer at the straw, and the rotting food and bones scattered amongst the wild flowers. Then, hopping inside a curious freshly-burrowed tunnel, she followed a rusty chain, which was attached to the wall until she stumbled across an iron, circus type cage in the darkness. Inside, a group of fairies were huddled together, tethered by a chain, the smallest of them whimpering in her sleep.

Shocked by the sight of the bedraggled fairies, the Princess whispered, *"Wand – on the count of three, you must set the little marsh fairies free – one, two, three,"* and with an almighty swish, the chain shattered into pieces. One by one, the raggedy fairies sat up, and quickly scrambling to their feet, they jumped down from the unlocked cage.

"Charlotte, who did this to you?" Princess Erin asked the little, whimpering fairy.

"Finbar forced us to dig a tunnel, so they could help themselves to the leprechaun's gold," she said, pointing out the overflowing sacks stashed neatly in the corner. "He's taken the caves above the mining village and now he wants the meadow back too," she whispered, her dewy eyes wide with fright.

Following the Princess, the bewildered fairies stumbled along the dark tunnel, until up ahead they saw a black shadow, holding a flickering torch aloft, come lumbering around the corner.

"It's Duke," the Princess gasped, recognising the overweight rat boy, his black teeth protruding under his waxy whiskers.

"Stop, where are you going?" Duke growled, the glow of the flaming torch resting upon the faces of the quivering fairies.

"Get out of my way, I'm setting these marsh fairies free." Princess Erin snapped bravely, trying to push by. Duke's giant whiskery shadow flickered on the curve of the tunnel and, holding his fat belly, he laughed in her face.. Then, his mood changed suddenly, and he boomed:

"The marsh fairies work, and for that we give them shelter!"

"They do not work for you, now get out of my way. You have no right to be in the lower meadow." The Princess's voice quaked with anger.

"Why not make me?" Duke smirked, and, barring their way down the tunnel, he cracked his tail like a whip.

Shaking in her tiny shoes, Charlotte snatched the sparkly wand sticking out from the Princess's pocket, and quickly placed it in her hand.

"Freeze," the Princess commanded, gripping the wand. Zapping Duke, she froze him, with his ugly smirk now stuck on his face.

"Quickly, the spell lasts just minutes," she warned. Squeezing passed the frozen rat, she sprinted down the tunnel and into daylight, followed by the cavalcade of fairies.

"Now fly for your lives," she cried, and, spreading their wings, all but poor Charlotte flitted like colourful butterflies. Turning, the Princess saw the little fairy flapping her wings pitifully. With dozens of grey-cloaked rat boys sprinting from the tunnel, she snatched the little fairy, and, wrapping her arms around her, she corkscrewed into the sky.

"I'm sure Erin is fine, but it'll be dark soon," said King Marty, organising a search party and trying not to worry everyone. Worried about Erin too, Shane kept Georgia, and the red and gold clad dwarf guardians, in his sight as he searched the meadow.

"Look," he called loudly, noticing a strange, black mass swirling across the sky towards them. "It's a storm! Quick, take shelter on the ground!" Georgia ordered the dwarf guardians, as the blackness swirled ever closer.

"No, wait, it's a swarm of swamp rats, and there's Erin, flying ahead. She's carrying something. it's a little fairy!" Shane yelled, running to the top of a hill. The exhausted marsh fairies fluttered to safety behind the dwarf guardians in the sky.

"Please, help the Princess, she can't hold onto Charlotte much longer," they panted.

"Keep going, don't stop until you reach the Palace!" Georgia cried, ushering them through. Then, drawing back their bows, they fired. The arrows hit their target, piercing the swamp rats flesh, and as they spun to the ground like broken helicopters, the dwarf guardians cheered. Charlotte slipped from the Princess's grasp and with her weak wings flapping and pink, raggedy dress billowing, she plunged to earth like a stone. Following the stricken fairy's cries, a swamp rat, with wings like flapping black sheets, swooped. Horrified, the Princess dived too and, jabbing her wand in the rat's eye, she caught the hysterical fairy and landed on Shane's outstretched palm. Placing the frightened fairies out of harm's way, Shane picked up his shovel and batted the squealing rat across the field.

The next day, the dwarf guardians brought Finbar to the Palace where, swishing his crimson cloak arrogantly, he stood on his hind legs and towered over the King.

"Who gave you the right to move into the meadow; you bullied the marsh fairies into stealing the leprechaun's gold? Speak now!" King Marty raged, covering his nose with a handkerchief to block out Finbar's stench.

"I'm sorry, I made a mistake. I didn't know the lower meadow was out of bounds, Your Majesty," he groveled.

"Is that all you have to say? What about the marsh fairies and the gold?" the King barked.

"Surely you don't think I'd imprison the marsh fairies, or make them steal? I will find out who's responsible though," he smirked, as if he was doing the King a favour.

"The Princess was in great danger. What have you got to say about that?" Finbar dropped to all fours and prowled around the hall.

"Duke was merely trying to reason with her, it was she who turned it into a drama," he snapped, showing his black teeth.

"You are a liar, Finbar. I will not tolerate your filth, your greed or your bullying. You and the rat boys will get out of the meadow today," the King said, looking in the rat boy's hard black eyes.

Finbar leapt forward, angered by the King's words, and quick as a flash, the dwarf guardians threw a rope and held the monstrous rat tight, his claws raking the air inches from the King's face.

"The meadow will be mine and I'll bury you and your kingdom of idiots again. Let's face it, the meddling Stranger is never coming back!" he roared, straining against the rope, his claws still raking.

"Don't be so sure. I could deliver you to the Stranger tomorrow if I wanted," barked the King with a false confidence, and with a click of his fingers, the dwarf guardians dragged the struggling Finbar through the gates and down the curly road, where, armed with swords and bows and arrows, the guardians chased the rat boys back to the tall, marshy wetlands, to the cheers of the meadowers.

"I'm so proud of how Erin rescued the marsh fairies all alone. She'd make an excellent advisor, and you could share all your problems. What do you think?" Queen Olivia asked her husband.

"I think our daughter would make an excellent queen," King Marty said, to his wife's surprise.

"What is it? You're making me very nervous," Princess Erin asked over breakfast the next day, noticing how strangely her parents were acting.

"It's time to celebrate our victory, by giving the meadowers a new queen," her father said, with a glint in his eye.

"You want me to be queen of the Magical Meadow?" Erin beamed.

"Yes, the meadowers look up to you. You are very brave, you would make an excellent queen," the King said.

"If you're sure that's what you want, then I will be honoured to be the next queen," said Erin, hugging them both.

Princess Erin's coronation took place on a glorious September day, a grand occasion with lanterns glowing throughout the Magical Meadow, and long, oak tables that groaned under a magnificent feast. There were fruit bowls, sandwiches, biscuits, creamy trifles, rich honey buns, and platters of surprise pies with tasty fillings, like chocolate, raspberry, or caramel, or disgusting fillings, like soggy vegetables, liquorice, or rum. There were fairy cakes so light you had to catch them, and frosted sugar wands, gooey honeycomb cups, curly road crunch, purple heather, popping candy and gallons of fairy wine.

And of course, a magnificent, white frosted, three-tiered coronation cake, piped in gold with a golden sugar crown on top.

The Princess wore a spectacular gown of emerald green, and her braided hair sparkled with silver threads as a snow-white winged fairy horse carried her along the twinkling route, swishing its tail with pride. And as she stepped down onto the wooden platform, King Marty proudly placed the gold, emerald encrusted crown on her head.

"Queen Erin," he announced, to a fanfare of trumpets.

"Queen Erin," the meadowers cried, throwing their hats in the air. And as the sun set over the Glendalough hills, the music and dancing began.

Chapter 9

The Truth

One second his gran was standing there, as plain as day, and the next a beautiful fairy was shimmering in her place.

"William, please listen," the fairy said, fluttering her paper-thin wings as she moved daintily around the cell. William? Only Gran called him William.

"It's me, I'm Gran, and I know it sounds ridiculous but I'm also Erin, the fairy queen of the Magical Meadow. I became a mortal a long time ago, to marry your pops," the fairy said, shuffling her feet uncomfortably as Billy continued to stare at her open-mouthed. The fairy moved closer. Her lips were moving but he seemed to have gone deaf, blackness swum in front of his eyes and her voice drifted further and further away.

"Patsy, quickly, some water," he heard her muffled voice say, and then the blackness engulfed him and he crashed to the floor. Patsy cradled his head and put a silver flask to his lips. Sipping the water slowly, he saw the fairy's green eyes peering into his face in a blurry haze. She didn't have any wrinkles around her eyes, and she didn't wear those funny little specs that made his gran look like a wise, old owl. She was young and beautiful and wore a glittery, silver ribbon in her blonde ponytail to match her shimmering dress, just like a fairy from a storybook.

"Make her go away, she's a liar! What have you done with Gran? Bring her back now!" Billy cried, pushing the flask away.

"I can't make her go away because she's telling ye the truth, Billy boy. I'm sorry, I know it's hard to hear but please believe me, I wouldn't lie to ye," Patsy said, putting a comforting arm around his shoulder.

"You left this note on the hallway table" the fairy said, smoothing a crumpled piece of paper and putting it in his hand. Billy, his face as white as a ghost read the note with a faraway look in his eyes.

"King Marty and Queen Olivia are missing," Patsy told the fairy.

"What, but I thought they were safe in the West of Ireland?" she sniffed, wiping away the glittery tears rolling down her cheeks.

"And ye're neighbour, ye know the one the kids called Ratty Nimrev, he is a rat boy. No wonder ye hated him on sight. Finbar sent him in case King Marty and Queen Olivia showed up, and it was ratty who talked Billy boy into stowing away on the ferry," Patsy gabbled, putting the fairy in the picture.

"No, he wouldn't have run away if I hadn't told him the story of St Kevin's healing well," she said, blowing her nose.

"Who are King Marty and Queen Olivia?" Billy butted in, looking at the fairy.

"Well, I'm not sure you want to know, you've had a shock," she said, batting her thick, black eyelashes.

"What can be worse than my gran being a fairy in disguise?" he asked.

"They're your **great** grandparents," she blurted out, looking worryingly at Patsy.

"What?! But how can they be, my gran is mega old so they must be ancient," Billy scoffed at the idea.

"Fairies don't age like humans, and some live forever, if they don't get killed," the fairy said, feeling quite insulted.

"Finbar knows you're coming, at least that bit makes sense," Billy said, watching her fluttering wings as he stuffed the crumpled note in his pocket.

"Right, so we'd better leg it then, before it's too late," Patsy said, jumping around and filling the awkward silence.

"It didn't take you long to pick up Billy's lingo, I see," the fairy laughed, handing Patsy a small pouch.

"Oh thank ye, ye're Majesty," he said, his blue eyes glinting at the sight of the fresh batch of gold dust inside the pouch.

"Now quickly, close ye're eyes, Billy boy, and wish us safely back with Tia," he said, scattering the gold dust willy nilly around him.

"Magic dust, free us three – to the safety of the oak tree," Patsy chanted as Billy squeezed his eyes shut, but, except for a fizzing, stuttering sound like a damp firework going out, nothing happened.

"Drat, what's wrong now?" Patsy fumed, stamping his foot and going quite red.

"The pouch was hidden in a flowerpot, maybe it's gotten a little damp, let me try," said the fairy, swishing her wand dramatically. *"Magic wand, free us three – to the safety of the oak tree,"* she chanted and with a flash and bang, a puff of smoke transported them outside.

"It worked, it worked," Patsy cried, his arms arched over his head, and his feet criss crossing as he danced an Irish jig.

"Er, not quite, looks like we're both out of practice," said the fairy, looking across the lake at the ghost ship bobbing in the moonlight.

"What do we do now?" Billy asked, laughing at Patsy, who stopped dancing as suddenly as he'd began when he saw the ghost ship.

"We'll just have to try again later," the fairy said, reaching out and flattening down Billy's sticky up hair.

"No stop it, please don't, Gran does that. You have wings and a wand and it's just too weird," Billy blurted, dodging her hand again.

"Sorry, William, you must call me Erin – it will be easier for you," said the fairy, looking quite hurt.

The night darkened suddenly, like something had blocked out the moon, and, looking up, they were shocked to see hundreds of grotesque, flapping shapes covering the sky.

"Wow, what kind of birds are they, and where did they come from?" Billy yelled over the deafening sound of the flock swooping around their heads.

"They're not birds, William, they're flying swamp rats! We must run to the ghost ship, now!" Erin screamed, and, grabbing his hand, she dragged him down the hill towards the shore. A flapping swamp rat knocked Patsy off his feet, and, picking up a stick, he threw it, hitting the squawking rat as it flew away.

"Keep running, William," Erin yelled, stopping to drag a shaken Patsy to his feet. Black wings flapping wildly, the frightening swamp rats hooked them with their claws and tried to lift them off their feet.

"Forget the ghost ship, we have to go now before they carry us back to the caves," Patsy screamed, hanging onto Erin as another screeching rat tried carrying her away.

"It won't work," yelled Billy, punching the flapping, terrifying, black shapes with both fists as they ripped his clothes.

"Billy, it's our only chance, look!" Patsy yelled, pointing to an alarming number of rat boys scurrying downhill, led by the monstrous Finbar, his distinctive crimson cloak flying in the moonlight.

Desperately trying to ignore the pandemonium, Billy stood dead still and closed his eyes.

"That's it, Billy boy, now wish us out of here," Patsy panted, throwing the gold dust into the air as the rat boys wriggled ever nearer across the shore.

Grabbing each of their hands, Billy wished as hard as he could.

"Magic dust, free us three – to the safety of the oak tree," he heard Patsy say. Suddenly, he was as light as a feather and the deafening squeals of swamp rats faded into the background.

"You're safe now, Billy." He heard Tia's gentle, whispering voice and, opening his eyes, he was relieved to see the gentle tree spirits fading in and out as they gathered to gawp at them.

"Wow, that was close," Billy said, stepping forward.

"Oops, careful, catch him quickly," said Tia, as his legs buckled beneath him.

Chapter 10

The Sea Merrow

A long time ago

Erin couldn't believe it. Shane was selling Mcloughlin's farm and leaving Ireland for good.

"Please don't go, we'll miss you," she begged, watching him turning the soil.

"It's not the same now with Ma and Da gone," he said, leaning on his shovel. A glint of red and gold caught their eye and practically tumbling from the sky, Georgia the dwarf guardian, landed on a grassy patch beside them.

"What is it?" Erin asked the flustered fairy.

"Please come quickly, Your Majesty, Finbar's back with dozens of rat boys, and they're destroying the meadow," she panted breathlessly.

It was too late; everywhere they looked, rat boys were scuttling around the meadow. The ever-changing dark fairies, the Pooka, this time disguised as white stallions, were flattening everything under their hooves. And with grey manes flying, they hounded the terrified meadowers to the Palace.

"We'll find the Stranger, he'll free the meadow again," they panted, barricading the gates.

"There are too many, and now they have the swamp rats and the pooka too, even the Stranger can't help us now," said Patsy sadly.

"Fly with your bows and arrows ready," Queen Erin ordered the dwarf guardians as they flew over the damaged meadow. The draped black wings of the cawing swamp rats hung like battered umbrellas from the silver leaved trees. The little bridge bowed dangerously in the middle and the water chariot smoldered in the middle of the lake. Suddenly, hundreds of flapping black wings engulfed them and, screeching loudly, the red and gold banner of dwarf guardians were chased by the vicious swamp rats back to the Palace.

"There is a deep sadness in your eyes. Is it the mortal boy that is troubling you?" Queen Olivia asked her daughter.

"Shane is leaving Ireland and I'll never see him again," Erin whispered, her face flushing bright pink.

"Do you love him?" her mother asked, and, surprised by her bluntness, Erin nodded.

"Then you must go with him."

"But it's not possible, he's a mortal, Mother," she cried, glittery tears slipping down her pretty face.

"There is a way for you to become a mortal too," her mother said, surprising her again.

"But what about you and father?" Erin cried.

"If Finbar stays, there is no future for us here, and if Shane can make you happy, then we'll be happy too," the Queen said tearfully.

Sad to see the meadower's crops trampled, their homes deserted, and the leprechaun's sacks emptied of gold, Shane waded angrily into the wetlands. Grabbing the tails of a handful of rat boys, he stuffed them wriggling into a sack and flung it into the lake. A black carpet swept through the tall grass, and before he had a chance to run, vicious rat boys scuttled over him, nibbling him and sinking their teeth into his skin.

"Ah, there goes Shane McLoughlin," the locals said, seeing him running, his hands clawing at his face trying to pull off the invisible rats.

"Sure, he was always a little bit odd," they said pityingly.

"What happened to you?" Erin gasped later in the day, shocked by the savage bites.

"Never mind, I'll be leaving Ireland in a week," he said, trying to smile.

"Are you leaving because of me?" Erin asked boldly.

"Yes," he said simply, looking at the ground.

"What if I told you there's a way we can be together?" she blurted.

"I'd say that I'd be the happiest man in the world," said Shane.

Later that day, the King and Queen told them the story of Clodagh, the sea merrow, who had the power to make Erin a mortal.

"Besotted by her beauty, a fisherman once captured Clodagh and hid her red cloak, so she'd forget all about her previous life," the King began.

"Then, after years of happy marriage, she found it and as soon as it was around her shoulders, she remembered. That day she ran away, dived into the sea and never saw her husband again."

"What happened to her?" Shane asked.

"She sits on a rock, far out at sea, where, combing her long hair, she lures fishermen to the rocks with her beautiful singing," said the King.

"What happened to her husband?" Erin asked, feeling a little sorry for him.

"He died of a broken heart. Every night, you can hear him calling her name across the Irish Sea. His cries, they say, are more painful than the banshee's," the Queen said.

"She may mistake you for a fisherman but if you love Erin, it's a chance you must take," the King warned Shane, making them shiver.

The next day, after two hours of sailing on the choppy Irish Sea, the merrow's voice cut through the air and they understood how she lured fishermen to the rocks. They saw her through the morning mist, sitting on a rock, her red cloak draped over a snow-white gown, trimmed with green and purple seaweed. Singing to her reflection in a mirror she combed her long blue/black hair. Turning, she stared with mocking dark eyes, and, raising her arms, she sang louder. An icy gale blew across the sea, giant waves battered the little boat and as thunder roared and lightning flashed, the merrow splashed into the sea. Shane struggled against the howling wind to look over the side of the boat, and, soaking them in freezing water, she crashed through the surf. Then, flipping her silver tail over the side, she climbed effortlessly from the sea.

"You're lucky to have survived. Now turn your boat around and never come back," she hissed, her dark stormy eyes almost turning Shane to stone.

"You don't understand, I want to be a mortal," Erin said. Startled, the merrow's eyes scanned the boat, her frightening gaze resting on Erin.

"My father, King Marty, sent us to you," she said, shivering and ruffling her saturated wings.

"Your father, why?" Clodagh hissed, outraged.

"He wants me to be happy," Erin replied.

"Your father wants you to become old and ugly," Clodagh said disgustedly.

"No, he wants me to have a new life," Erin said bravely.

"But you will lose your beauty and eventually die," Clodagh said, her silvery tail swishing agitatedly.

"The rat boys have taken the Magical Meadow, we can't find the Stranger and there is no one else to help us," Erin explained.

"How can you be sure that's what you want?" Clodagh hissed, with a look of disgust on her face.

"I know that I love Shane and that I want to marry him," Erin snapped, fed up with the stroppy merrow.

"You must have questions you need to ask me?" Clodagh asked, slithering around the boat.

"Well, yes, I have. Will I be able to remember my previous life?" Erin asked nervously.

"I have no idea about that," Clodagh said, shaking her head dismissively.

"Oh, well, if you were to grant my wish, would I become a young woman? I'm quite old in fairy years."

"Yes, yes, you will start your mortal life as a young woman but time will rob you of your youth," Clodagh said.

"Now, any more questions?" she barked, her eyes narrowing as she looked at Shane. Flustered, and unable to think of a single thing, Erin shook her head.

"Well, off with you then, and if you have any sense I will never see you again," Clodagh said, plunging into the icy, cold sea before Shane could utter a word.

"The meadow stinks, swamp rats are waiting in the trees like vultures, the Pooka trot around as if they own the place, and Finbar wants us out of the Palace by tomorrow," King Marty told them sadly on their return.

"You mean he was here? Did he hurt you?" Erin asked.

"No, but tomorrow they will be back to knock the gates down," the King shrugged, putting his head in his hands.

"We must go now, we'll go to the tree spirits they'll never find us in the oak tree," Erin said.

"No, you'll never be free you must go with Shane and start a new life," her mother sobbed.

"You and Father must come too, we can start a new life together," Erin said.

"You are young, we are too old for such a change, but some of the meadowers would like to go with you," her mother said, trying to cheer her up.

Early the next day, accompanied by the King and Queen, Erin and Shane set sail to find Clodagh again. Crashing frighteningly through the surf, the merrow climbed on board and slithered around the deck.

"So, Queen Erin, you have chosen a mortal life," she said. As if impatient to get it over with, she handed Erin a mirror and began to sing. "♫♫ *Erin, shed your fairy guise in exchange for a mortal life - to live forever as Shane's wife* ♫♫." Her beautiful voice drifted over the Irish Sea, and a mist swirled around them. Then, placing her snow-white hands on Erin's head, she repeated the words/

"*Erin, shed your fairy guise in exchange for a mortal life – to live forever as Shane's wife.*"

Rays of sunshine stabbed the mist, Erin's legs began to tingle, and a bolt of lightning helter-skeltered around her body.

"Remember, the spell will be broken if you ever return to Glendalough." Clodagh spoke now to the green-eyed, flaxen-haired, beautiful young woman standing beside Shane.

"Do you mean the spell will be broken if I return?" Erin whispered, staring at the familiar green eyes in her unfamiliar face in the mirror.

"You didn't ask enough questions!" Clodagh cackled, diving from the rocking boat into the Irish Sea and leaving them softly weeping.

Chapter 11

Beltenor and Ronan

So badly shaken, Billy was afraid to go outside. "I want to go home now, the flying rats wanted to kill us," he cried, pacing around the oak tree.

"Don't worry, we'll find someone to help us, you want your mammy to get better don't ye?" Patsy said, trying to cheer him up.

"She's my mum, not my mammy," Billy said, irritated by Patsy, who always pronounced it wrong.

"Well, in Ireland she's your mammy whether ye like it or not," Patsy scoffed.

"Well, Patsy, you're very bold," Erin said, knowing how terrified he was of the rat boys.

"I don't want Billy boy to go home empty handed. Do ye know of anyone who could help us, Tia?" he asked.

"Um, er, yes," the dreamy tree spirit answered, barely taking her eyes off Erin the fairy queen, who she could hardly believe was back after all these years.

"What about the water witch, do you remember her?"

"Of course, you mean Beltenor," Erin and Patsy piped up together.

"Yes, but we must speak to her guardian first because she's so grand these days. It's he who decides whether we're worthy or not," Tia said.

"Do you think we're worthy?" Billy asked, excited by the sound of the water witch.

"We'll soon find out, that's if you want to," Erin said.

"Beltenor sounds wicked, how do we find her?" he beamed, nodding eagerly and forgetting all about the swamp rats.

"We'll leave that to Tia, she'll show us the way," said Erin, not at all surprised by his change of heart.

Guiding them to the beach, Tia told them they were in luck. It was the last Friday of the month and Beltenor's guardian was due to appear on the wild, grassy dunes of Brittas Bay.

"It's definitely Friday today, isn't it?" Billy asked, trying to work the days out on his fingers.

"Will ye stop fretting," Patsy said impatiently, secretly counting the days himself.

"Beltenor's guardian is said to have a dark secret. Why else would he live under the sea with Beltenor? She's so demanding," Tia said, shivering as a cold wind whipped across the beach.

A stocky figure, holding a rusty sword in his hand, suddenly appeared and surprised to see the odd-looking group, he stepped backwards, making his rusty armour clang loudly.

"Ahem, ahem, greetings. I am Ronan, guardian to the wise water witch, Beltenor," he said, his striking blue eyes blinking through a rusty face guard.

"Nice to meet you," Erin said, trying not to giggle. The rusty guardian wasn't at all what she'd expected.

"Well, how can I help you?" he snapped, shuffling his feet as they continued to stare.

"I'm the fairy queen of the Magical Meadow and this is William, Patsy, and Tia," she said, introducing the shivering, little party.

"We are searching for St Kevin's well. William's mother, who is my daughter, is very sick, and the water is said to be healing. We believe it is above the mining village and we need some help to get to the caves," she finished, wondering why he was frowning at her.

"If you know where the well is said to be, why bother Beltenor at all?" Ronan snapped.

"The caves are over-run by rat boys," Erin said, not liking his attitude.

"Rat boys? They were banished to the wetlands by the Stranger," Ronan barked, stepping closer to Erin.

"Yeah, don't s'pose you know where to find him, do you?" Billy butted in.

"Silence! Shall I tell Beltenor that the half-mortal fairy queen, who deserted the Magical Meadow, needs help?" he smirked, taking another step closer. Erin's face was red with anger and Billy suddenly felt sorry for Ronan as she stepped closer still.

"We were driven from the meadow because we were outnumbered by Finbar, the rat boys, the pooka and the swamp rats, and because no one else cared. Maybe, if you hadn't cowered under the sea you'd have known that. You stupid rust bucket of a guardian," she spat furiously. Billy, Tia and Patsy shuffled uncomfortably and Ronan, wounded by her words, looked down at his rusty seaweed-strewn armour. Then, gripping his rusty sword, he turned to face the sea. *"Sea, make way,"* he boomed over the tumbling, crashing waves.

The sea split straight down the middle with a thunderous crash, leaving huge, steel grey walls of seawater, tumbling and gurgling either side of a slippery path.

"Quickly, follow me and you'll be able to breathe like fish. However, if you are wasting my time, the walls will crash and seal you under the sea forever," he warned. And even though Ronan looked like an idiot, Billy was sure that given half a chance he'd make the deafening, sea walls sweep them away.

Shivering with fear as well as the freezing sea spray, they picked their way around jellyfish, shells and seaweed, and followed Ronan down a never-ending path to where a magnificent castle was quivering at the bottom like a giant, transparent jelly. *"Settle,"* Ronan bellowed, turning his back. With a terrifying force, the monstrous walls collapsed, sealing them into Beltenor's strange, under-water world with a thunderous roar.

Slurping oysters, cockles, mussels and shrimps, Beltenor pushed back her waist-length, auburn hair, eyed them curiously, and carried on eating. And sitting nervously on the high back shell chairs that Ronan had ushered them to, they watched the sea life swim by the transparent walls and waited for the underwater diva to finish.

"I know nothing of this healing well," she said dismissively in a strange, musical voice after hearing their story.

"Except, I did meet an old mortal fisherman in a cave many moons ago, who was looking for a well."

"Oh, but then he died," she sang, crushing their hopes as she examined her perfect fingernails. "He mentioned a map and a key before he, um, popped off though," she added, coyly looking at Patsy under her eyes.

"Excuse me, did you say a key?" Billy butted in, making Beltenor's exquisite eyes whirl like Catherine wheels, changing from sea blue to green, to grey, then to turquoise. Darting like tiny, silver fishes, several pretty water nymphs combed her hair to calm her down.

"There is a key to unlock the healing well," she quoted the fisherman, "and then he was gone," she said, with a snap of her fingers.

"He was a mortal, so it isn't just a fairy tale. Did he say where the key was hidden?" Billy badgered, infuriating her again.

"No, that dreadful Captain Nealy and his shabby crew came along. And besides, he'd popped his clogs by then," she said, exasperated, as the water nymphs frantically fanned her with black and white swan's feathers.

"Excuse me, Beltenor, would ye be able to suggest a way to get near the caves? Finbar and the rat boys are crawling all over the Glendalough hills," Patsy said in his most charming voice, while glaring at Billy.

"Isn't he just adorable?" Beltenor cooed at Patsy. "You should stay with me, then you need never worry about the nasty rat boys again. Everyone should have a leprechaun, they bring you such good luck," she said, tickling Patsy's beard with her long, red talons and making him blush.

"Good luck! Don't make me laugh, I've been hunted, captured by ugly rats, locked in a cage and crushed by shingle dragons. Even his wishes are rubbish," Billy scoffed.

"Well, I didn't hear you complaining when a wish mended the pot," Patsy snapped.

"I set you free from that pot, don't forget," Billy snapped back.

"Beltenor doesn't want to listen to your silly arguments," Erin hissed, noticing the diva's eyes whirling again.

"Those filthy rats belong in the wetlands, and I promise I will give them my full attention when I have more time," Beltenor yawned, as if exhausted.

Time was one thing Beltenor seemed to have plenty of, but Erin thanked her anyway and, with her eyes now settled to calm, sea green, Beltenor leaned forward.

"I have an idea," she said, dabbing her ruby red lips on a napkin.

"Why not take Ronan, my guardian, for one week? He's clumsy, but he's ever so brave."

"One week, that's no good," Billy cried, enraging her again.

"Please forgive him, Beltenor. William is worried about his mother, a week is more than generous, thank you," Erin said, putting an arm protectively around Billy and giving him a pinch.

"Ouch," he said.

"You can be very aggravating, young man. One week is all I can spare, besides, who would deal with my public. Ronan, fetch the sea horses," Beltenor shrilled, fixing Billy with a watery, grey stare.

Chapter 12

The Forest of Darkness

Ronan's armour squeaked every time he shoveled down a spoonful of Evie's gooseberry pie, setting everyone's teeth on edge.

"Sure, leave it to me," Patsy winked, "and I'll have a wee, gentle, word in his ear."

"Ronan," he barked, "ye're creaking like an 'auld' (old) barn door, the rat boys will hear ye a mile off."

Still wounded by Erin's 'rusty bucket' comment, Ronan reluctantly handed it to the tree spirits for a sprucing up. Annoyed at Patsy for being so brutal, Tia, Evie, Molly and Wisp first oiled the rusty armour, and then they rubbed it with bark shavings and buffed it with sheep's wool, until it sparkled like new.

"What about the helmet?" Tia asked.

"I want to keep it on," said Ronan.

"But it'll look odd," she said, confused.

"Then polish it on my head," Ronan snapped. And so, as his fearful blue eyes peered through the face guard, the rusty old helmet got the same treatment. Ronan was over the moon. He felt great not to be dripping with salty water and slimy seaweed, and not to have to eat raw fish every day.

Billy whistled. "The tree spirits have done a wicked job," he told Patsy.

"He'll blind everyone for miles around," the leprechaun laughed, shielding his eyes from the dazzling guardian.

"We'll use him to frighten the rat boys with their own ugly mugs," they agreed, watching Ronan admiring his reflection in a wonky, oak framed mirror.

"We'll take this trail around the upper lake, through the pinewoods and into the Forest of Darkness." Ronan said stabbing the map, spread on the oak table, with a finger.

"Only the brave, or very stupid, go through the Forest of Darkness," Patsy snapped, surprised by his master plan.

"Besides, the Dark Man won't allow us to cross it," Tia said, horrified.

"Who's he?" Billy asked, his ears pricking up.

"He hasn't been seen for years," Ronan said.

"He rides his black-winged horse through this forest, I've seen him," Tia insisted.

"But that's impossible," Ronan said.

"How would you know, you live under the sea?" she said, annoyed he didn't believe her.

"Er, who's the Dark Man?" Billy repeated, putting his hand up.

"I heard he's wary of the Stranger too," Ronan said, ignoring him.

"Please tell me who the dark man is," Billy whined impatiently.

"He's a dark fairy. He lived in the Forest of Darkness for many years," Erin said.

"So, he's mean then?" Billy said, not happy with yet another problem.

"Yes, especially to children," Erin said.

"Oh, that's just great," said Billy.

"Sorry, but one little boy hasn't spoken a word since he stumbled across him, and some children haven't been seen since," Tia said.

"Look, Billy will be safe with me. Besides,, he's more like a little meadower," Ronan laughed, ruffling Billy's hair.

"How come the children could see him?" Billy asked.

"The Dark Man takes only the children with the gift of sight," Patsy said, making him gulp.

"What about the truds that live in the mud pits?" Tia asked.

"Er, what's a trud?" Billy asked, not fancying a trek through the dark forest at all.

"Truds are mud trolls, and they won't bother you unless you bother them. Let's look on the bright side, there are no rat boys in the forest," Ronan said, giving Tia an icy, blue stare.

"No, that's because they're scared of the Dark Man, and the truds too," said Billy, making them laugh.

Flushed after their long climb, they looked down at the silvery upper lake.

"Are we near the Forest of Darkness?" Billy asked.

"Nope, this is St Kevin's bed," Patsy said, showing him around a small cave.

"Wow, where's his bed then?" Billy asked, wandering around the bare, tiny space.

"It's not a real bed, silly," Erin said, slapping a stone slab.

"You mean he slept on that?" Billy asked, disappointed.

"Well his abode mightn't have much furniture but it certainly has a great view," said Patsy, watching the boats carrying day-trippers up and down the calm lake. Erin and Tia linked Billy's arms, and, feet kicking, they flew him over the sparkling waterfalls, purple mountains, and green fields, spattered with horses, cows and sheep, all grazing lazily.

"Is this the Forest of Darkness then?" he asked, stomach lurching as they dropped in between two sooty black trees. Ronan pushed through the undergrowth and, following him, they stumbled into complete blackness. The forest guardians darted around, the peacock blue light illuminating the black, gnarled trees with coal, black leaves blocking out the warmth of the sun, as well as the twisted, black brambles, the drooping, black flowers, and the charred black leaves that crunched under their feet as they walked further into the forest.

The forest guardians looked amazing, twinkling amongst the black trees of the sad, lonely forest like little blue diamonds. Hearing Erin calling softly, Billy realised he'd wandered too far and, turning, he stumbled into a gurgling, black mess.

"Help, something is holding my ankles!" he yelled, swirling around in a black pit as if someone had pulled out the plug.

"Grab the rope," Ronan yelled, throwing it quickly. Billy fished around, grabbing the end, his screams turning to gurgles as his mouth filled with the sticky mud. Erin, Patsy, and Tia heaved the rope with Ronan until at last, Billy shot out of the pit, smothering them in mud.

"Something is in there," he gasped, spewing out black gunge and wiping it from his eyes. An almighty 'roar' filled the darkness, and out of the pit climbed a huge muddy creature, with small eyes and a big mouth, dripping gloopy mud everywhere.

"Stand back, it's a trud," said Ronan, as the muddy creature towered over them, boxing the flitting forest guardians. Then, reaching out, it lifted Patsy off his feet.

"Help, help," Patsy squealed, trying to wriggle out of his jacket with Erin clinging to his coattail. Dangling Patsy in front of its mouth, the trud flicked her off like a bug. Ronan swished his sword like a musketeer and, springing upwards, he stabbed the truds muddy fist again and again, until wounded, it dropped his head on Patsy. Then, cascading downwards like a chocolate fountain, the trud dissolved into a muddy puddle.

"That monster nearly had me for its dinner because of ye," Patsy snapped, bashing his dented hat back into shape.

"I'm sorry, Patsy; I didn't see the pit," Billy explained, tears pricking the back of his eyes.

"Just stay with us, it's simple," Patsy raged, going red in the face and stomping off.

"I didn't mean it," whined Billy pathetically.

Before they had a chance to say another word, horses' hooves thundered through the forest, shaking the earth.

"Quick, this way," said Ronan, disappearing into the thick, black undergrowth. The whinnying horse slowed to a trot and the rider dismounted. Footsteps crunched over the leaves, and then stood still in the darkness.

"*I smell a leprechaun, a tree spirit and a boy, come out now and show yourselves to the Dark Man,*" he boomed, sniffing the air menacingly.

Ronan climbed out first, and the guardian's wings shed light on a scary monk-like figure draped in a black, hooded cloak.

"I know you from somewhere," he thundered, as Ronan stroked the horse's black mane.

"I'm Ronan, guardian to Beltenor, the water witch," he answered.

"And before that?" barked the terrifying Dark Man.

"I did many things, mainly combat," Ronan shrugged.

"What happened to you, boy, why are you so small?" he growled, stepping towards Billy and making him shiver.

"Finbar shrunk me," he said miserably.

"Finbar? Where did you meet that smelly flea bag?" he asked.

"In the caves, when he captured us, but we escaped because Patsy's wish worked for once," Billy said.

Patsy was about to argue when, to their surprise, the Dark Man burst out laughing.

"Well, that's quite an adventure for a little boy. Why are you crossing the Forest of Darkness?" he asked.

"We're searching for St Kevin's healing well. Have you heard of it?" Billy asked him.

"I know nothing about the healing well, but I can offer you a ride on this beautiful horse. It belonged to the real Dark Man," he said, holding the reins of the jittery horse while it nuzzled Ronan's hand.

And, pushing back his hood, he revealed a shock of ginger hair.

"Ah, the Red-haired Man," said Ronan.

"Everyone is scared of the Dark Man, so you must see why it's quite a useful disguise," he laughed, as they breathed a sigh of relief.

"What happened to this beautiful forest?" Erin asked him.

"The rat boys burnt it to the ground and cursed it to remain in darkness forever," he said.

"Finbar and the Dark Man were as thick as thieves, it doesn't make sense," Tia said.

"They quarreled and then the Dark Man disappeared," the Red haired Man said.

"Why do you live here?" she asked.

"The rat boys don't bother with the forest, and as long as I avoid the truds, it's a great place to live. I just hope the Dark Man never comes back," he said, helping them up onto the horse. The shiny, black horse galloped, snorting, through the forest, and then, flapping its magnificent, leathery wings, it soared over the black treetops and across the starry, black sky. Feeling the rush of the wind, it carried them the length of the forest before landing on the charred black earth on the other side.

The Red-haired Man pointed the way through two sooty, black trees. "Through there is the miner's village, you'll find the caves at the top of the hill, behind the granite rocks," he said.

"Why don't you come with us?" Billy asked.

"No, the forest may be bathed in sunlight one day, and I don't want to miss it. Oh, but I nearly forgot, just blow if you need my help," he said, handing Ronan a slim, silver, whistle. "It won't make a sound but I will hear you. Good luck with the healing well," he said, grinning at Billy, who'd told him the whole story on the way. Ronan patted the horse's nose.

"I think the horse took a shining to you, Ronan," Patsy said, listening to its painful whinnying as the Red-haired Man led it away.

Chapter 13

Searching for the Healing well

They picked their way across the amazing, ghostly miner's village, with its mounds of twinkling rocks, skeletons of stone buildings, and a relic of a rusty mill wheel. Billy couldn't resist popping some glistening rocks in his pocket.

"Wow, what's that?" he asked, staring into a deep, black hole as they stepped inside the entrance of the first cave.

"It's not the healing well, there's no water down there," said Ronan, listening to the distant thud of the glistening rock that Billy dropped into the blackness.

"Who knows what the rat boys are up to?" he shrugged.

"Billy, you stay here and search with Erin and Tia," Ronan said, taking charge.

"Why? I want to go with you," he whined.

"I think it's best if you let Patsy get over the trud episode, the rat boys are never far and I don't want you two arguing," Ronan said, watching the leprechaun kicking stones in a classic sulk.

"But he won't even speak to me," Billy said, annoyed he had to stay with the girls.

"Nevertheless, I think it's best. We won't be long," said Ronan, already striding into the cave.

Patsy brazenly zoomed down a giant, bumpy slide into the belly of the cave. Wishing Billy was with him, he tapped the walls and searched the dark crevices of the spooky alleyway. Following the sandy path between the giant rocks, he stumbled across a big, fat rat boy asleep outside a huge, stone door. And with his heart beating like a drum, he tiptoed past and bravely pushed it open.

Almost at the top of the huge wall, a shadow crept over Ronan. Looking up, he saw a huge, slathering swamp rat above his head. Screeching, as it flapped its lacy, black wings wildly, it swooped, and hooking him with its sharp talons, it rattled him like a tin can. Struggling to cling on, Ronan lashed out with his sword until the swamp rat flapped away, and, swinging his legs upwards, he scrambled on to the flat surface.

The swamp rat's squeals echoed around the cave as it swooped down again, and, wrapping Ronan in its black wings, it dragged him to the edge. Freeing his arm, Ronan lashed out with his sword again, and screeching as if in pain, it flapped upwards the mighty draught from its powerful wings blowing him over. It circled the roof of the cave, its wings slowing and its ebony eyes watching, before attacking again, and as it swooped onto the ledge, Ronan grabbed the swamp rat around the neck. With its wings thrashing wildly, they fought in a cloud of dust. Breaking free, the swamp rat pounced, its dagger-sharp teeth and talons ready, Ronan staggered backwards, and, raising his sword, he brought it down sharply, slicing the swamp rat's wing in two. With blood spraying everywhere, they rolled over the edge into the deep gorge.

"I thought they wouldn't be long," said Billy, miffed that they hadn't found the well, and at being left with the girls for what felt like hours. Wandering further into the cave, he heard a soft murmur, like someone in pain. "Ronan?" he called, throwing himself flat on his belly and peering into the gorge. 'Is that you?'

"Billy…" Ronan answered from the blackness.

Billy slid downwards, over the bumpy surface, the panicking forest guardians flitting around him like blue shooting stars.

"Are you hurt?" he panted, kneeling beside Ronan, who was squashed underneath the heavy swamp rat, blood oozing everywhere.

"No, I'm fine, it's the rat's blood," Ronan croaked, barely able to breathe.

"Wand as quick as that," Erin chanted, *"free Ronan from underneath the swamp rat."* And, in a puff of smoke, the rat disappeared.

"Where's Patsy?" Ronan asked, gratefully clanging to his feet.

"We were hoping you'd tell us that," Erin said, relieved the only damage seemed to be a couple of dents in his armour.

"How do you know that Patsy came this way?" Billy asked, following Ronan, their shadows dancing on the walls like blue phantoms from the light cast by the forest guardians' wings.

"I don't think the rat boys wear hobnail boots, do you?" Ronan said, following the tiny boot prints in the sand.

"Quickly, the rat boys may know that we're in the cave by now," he added, pushing open a stone door to reveal a warren of alleyways.

"Oh no, what now?" Billy whispered.

"Hurry, we'll try them all," said Ronan, drawing his sword.

Ronan carefully pushed open another door at the end of the first alleyway, to find piles of dirty rags littered all over the floor.

"That pile just moved," Tia whispered, grabbing Erin's hand.

"I saw it move too," said Billy, stepping behind them. Flipping his sword, Ronan caught the blade and jabbed the pile with the blunt end.

"Arrrrgh," a voice groaned, making them jump.

He prodded it again.

"Ouch, get off me!" a voice snapped and, flipping his sword, he pointed it at the wriggling bundle.

A little, muddy face popped out and, scrubbing her eyes, the marsh fairy stared at the tip of the sword.

"Patsy, Patsy, where are you?" Billy called, suddenly getting very excited,

"Sssshhh," Ronan hissed crossly, clamping his hand over Billy's mouth.

"Billy boy, is that you?" Patsy answered, to everyone's surprise. And, breaking free, Billy ran blindly into the room, colliding with Patsy into the darkness.

"Are you okay?" Billy asked, rubbing his head,

"Absolutely fine, Billy boy," said Patsy, seeing stars, and forgetting they'd fallen out over the trud, they swung each other around.

"What's all the noise about?" someone snapped from the other end of the room,

"Donal?" Patsy said, recognising the voice.

"Patsy? Is that you?" he replied. Tiny lanterns lit up around them one by one illuminating their dingy surroundings.

"Patsy, my dear cousin," a whiskery, bald chap gasped, blowing his nose on a handkerchief.

"It's Erin, the Fairy Queen," the meadowers muttered, popping from under the raggedy piles, wondering if they were dreaming.

"Charlotte, Georgia, I thought you'd left Glendalough?" Erin gasped, as her two bedraggled friends stepped into the light.

"Finbar stopped us a long time ago," Georgia, the dwarf guardian, said sadly.

"What happened to King Marty and Queen Olivia?" Erin asked.

"Finbar threatened to separate them, and one day they vanished," said Charlotte, the little marsh fairy.

"How did you get out of that pot?" Donal laughed, poking Patsy to make sure he was real.

"Let's just say I was dropped on my head," Patsy laughed, winking at Billy.

"Finbar stuffed him in the pot and hurled him into the Irish Sea, and if Shane hadn't fished him out on the day they were leaving, goodness knows what would've happened," Donal told Billy, as if it was yesterday.

"The door isn't locked, we should go while we have the chance," said Billy, feeling a bit uneasy.

"I couldn't find my way out of the room. I thought I was alone," said Patsy, recognising the grubby pixies, gnomes, elves and leprechauns gathering under the lantern.

"That lazy fat guard must have forgotten to lock it. Quickly, before they come back!" said Donal, holding the door open.

"Too late! Stand aside, you useless shoe mending idiot," Finbar growled, shoving Donal flat on his back. And, tail sweeping the floor, he scurried into the room, followed by a dozen smelly rat boys. The meadowers fled to the dark corners and, quickly blowing a kiss to Billy, Tia vanished along with the forest guardians.

"Well, well, a reunion, how touching," Finbar smirked, striding around on two legs while the other rat boys prowled around, sniffing their clothes.

"Don't you recognise your neighbour, Queenie?" he barked at Erin, as the fat rat boy to his side began to fizzle, and crackle, and shed his fur in clumps, revealing her trusted neighbour Ratty Nimrev, with a thick mat of fur at his feet and with smoke billowing out of his ears.

"You!" Erin gasped.

"I thought perhaps King Marty and Queen Olivia had come to you. It was me who persuaded the brat to stowaway to Ireland, knowing that you'd follow. It won't be long now until your precious mother and father will come rushing back too," he laughed. Then, pulling up his fur like a onesie, he became the equally loathsome Nimrev again. "Welcome back to your kingdom of half-wits, Your Majesty," Finbar chuckled evilly.

"If I had known how cruelly you'd treated the meadowers I'd have come back sooner. You won't get away with this, Finbar," Erin snapped.

"And who are you?" Finbar barked, turning to Ronan and ignoring Erin.

"Ronan, guardian to Beltenor," he said.

"Remove your helmet, I'd like to see your face. Have you no manners?" Finbar growled, showing his needle-sharp black teeth.

"It's stuck," said Ronan, struggling with the helmet and pretending to twist it around.

"Remove it now or I'll cut off your head," Finbar snapped, and before Ronan knew what was happening, Finbar yanked the helmet from his head.

"Oooh," cried the meadowers, shocked by Ronan's scaly, blue fish head staring at the floor.

"Oh, on second thoughts you'd better put it back on!" Finbar roared, throwing the helmet back to him. Then, still laughing, he snatched Ronan's sword and Erin's wand and swept through the cell door, followed by the other laughing rat boys.

"Where's Tia?" Ronan asked, quickly putting the helmet back on.

"She vanished with the guardians ages ago," Billy whispered in shock.

"Good, she'll be looking for a way out," he said, relieved she hadn't seen his ugly fish head.

"Did Beltenor do that to you?" Erin asked.

"No, it was the Sea Merrow, she gave me a choice of drowning or this," he shrugged, tapping the tin helmet.

"Wow, no wonder you live under the sea," Billy said, trying to catch another glimpse of the blue scales through his face guard.

"William, don't be so rude," Erin snapped.

"Can it be undone?" Patsy asked.

"Yes, in a hundred years or so, or when I've achieved something of greatness," Ronan shrugged.

That night, unable to sleep for thinking about the healing well and Ronan's blue fish head, Billy grabbed a lantern and went to explore the caverns around the dingy room. Disappointed to find only dead ends, he was on his way back when, startled by a whirring sound, he dropped the lantern with a clang. A door creaked in the darkness, and quickly blowing out the lantern, he ducked behind a rock.

"What was that?" a voice whispered.

"I don't know, but don't light the lantern dummy," someone snapped, and the door closed again.

"What?! You went off on your own? What if Finbar had found you wandering around in the middle of the night?" Erin snapped furiously when Billy told what he'd heard the next morning.

"Ahh don't worry that'll be Captain Nealy and his crew from the ghost ship. They're planning our escape," Donal said, overhearing.

"Why? Aren't pirates bad?" Billy asked, confused.

"Well, yes, but they've had their inner phantoms cut out, they can't even remember where they buried the treasure. That's why every day Finbar has us digging up a different part of the cave," Donal explained.

"They've had what cut out?" Billy asked.

"Never mind, let's go and meet them," Donal said.

"Will they know where the healing well is?" Billy asked.

"It's not likely, if they can't even remember where they buried the treasure," Ronan shrugged.

Donal gave four, sharp taps, a concealed door slid open with a creek and a black bearded pirate, wearing a pirate's hat, trimmed with red feathers, a blue and white striped shirt, breeches and black swashbuckling boots, with a black patch over his right eye peeped out.

"Top of the morning," said Captain Nealey, showing his black teeth and looking at them with his roving left eye.

"Ah, so it was you creeping about," he laughed when they explained about the night before.

"Dick, Ted, uncover the wheel, the boy wants to see what we're up to. Move, this is royalty we 'ave 'ere," he said, taking off his hat and bowing to Erin. A red bearded, peg-legged pirate, with a purple bandana wrapped around his straggly, red hair, and a pirate in a green bandana, with a yellow beard, uncovered the strange object in the corner of the bare room, while the scruffy crew, all wearing bandanas of a different colour, jumped to their feet.

"Ta dah! We made it ourselves," said the Captain proudly, running his fingers through his black beard.

"It's a wheel," said Erin, confused.

"It's not just any old wheel," the Captain said indignantly, unveiling buckets of gold dust underneath it.

"It's a grinding wheel, we grind gold for the little munchkins so they can make wishes and magic," he laughed.

"But that's brilliant," Erin squealed. "where did you find the gold?"

"Do you know, I can't remember," he said, looking at the crew all shaking their heads.

"Don't I know you?" the Captain asked Ronan, changing the subject and standing back to have a good look at him.

"I live under the sea, it's possible," Ronan said.

"I think you'd remember him, he's got a blue fish head underneath that helmet," said Billy.

"William!" snapped Erin.

"Hmmm, don't recall anyone with a blue fish head," said the Captain, his roving eye looking him up and down.

"Captain, do you know where to find St Kevin's healing well? It might be in this cave," Billy asked him.

"Well, little un, I'll have a think about that," he said and, still watching Ronan, he showed them to the door.

Chapter 14

The map and the key

"Trying to snatch the keys is impossible. The rat boys are always passing them around, and their cloaks stink," Tia said, reappearing like a ghost in the room and making them laugh.

"Tia, Captain Nealy doesn't remember anything about the healing well," Billy told her disappointedly.

"The captain of the ghost ship is here? But that's brilliant, doesn't he have a ship's diary?" she asked.

"I didn't ask him that," said Billy, his eyes lighting up. Before they could stop him, he was banging on the Captain's door again.

"Ahhhh, I think I jot our adventures down in this scribbling book," the Captain said, and, taking a wad of pages tied with string from a shelf, he flicked through them.

"Oh there you are, my dear," he said, startled by Tia's disappearing habit and finding her hovering hazel eyes quite unnerving.

"It says 'ere, that an old fisherman gave me a map marking a well inside this cave," he beamed, stabbing a page with his finger.

"Yes, I remember now," he said, following the scribbling. "That hoity toity Beltenor was 'ere, and she thought he'd popped his clogs, but after she'd gone he gave me a map. We buried him at sea, and I took a necklace to his brother's farm," he read, raising an eyebrow as if surprised by his own honesty.

"But ah hah, I kept the map," he said, underlining the words with his finger, obviously pleased to read that he was still a bit of a rogue.

"Did he say anything about a key?" Erin asked.

"Yes, there's a drawing of a key on the map," he said, triumphantly flicking through his notes again.

"But where is the map, Captain?" Billy asked, bursting with excitement.

"Oh no," he said, licking his thumb and turning the page. "After years of mislaying it, I buried it with the treasure for safe keeping."

"What?!" Billy exploded. "You buried the map with the treasure! The lost treasure! The 'nobody knows where it is' treasure!" he cried, hardly able to believe his rotten luck.

"Calm down, the meadowers will find it, there can't be many places left to dig up," said the Captain, giving Billy a curious look.

"You've been very helpful, Captain," Erin said, and, grabbing Billy's hand, they rushed off to find Ronan, wishing they'd never asked.

Before they had a chance to explain about the map, the rat boys put Ronan and Patsy to work digging for the treasure.

"What's going on?" Tia asked, appearing alongside them, wondering about the excitement as rat boys scurried everywhere.

"I think we've just dug up the treasure," Ronan said, watching the greedy rat boys wriggling all over the wooden trunk hoisted from its grave.

"The Captain says the map, marking the whereabouts of the healing well, is buried with that treasure," Tia said, excited.

"Oh, ingenious," said Patsy, knee deep in dirt. "And how are we supposed to get to it now?" Several crowbar-wielding rat boys prized the mud-caked treasure trove open, revealing sparkling emeralds, sapphires, rubies, diamonds and pearls, nestling amongst silver and gold trinkets. Duke strutted around, with a diamond tiara on his head and handkerchief under his snout.

"I am the Queen, has anyone seen my kingdom?" he said, in a mocking high-pitched voice. Finbar leapt from rock to rock with a hideous smirk and, swiping the tiara from Duke's head, he threw it in the trunk.

"Bring the treasure to my nest," he ordered the weary meadowers, who were up to their necks in the dirt. "I need to go over my plans for these useless meadowers," and, brushing past the unseen Tia, he scampered into the darkness.

"Billy, they've found the treasure," Tia whispered, unlocking the stone door of their room with keys she'd just snatched from Finbar's belt.

"We don't have time for Captain Nealy's crackpot stories, there's no time to look for a map," Ronan said gruffly, following her into the room with Patsy.

"Don't you believe the Captain's story?" Tia asked.

"He can hardly remember his name," Ronan argued.

"At least with a map, we'll have a chance," she bristled.

"Finbar has no further use for the meadowers now that he's found the treasure, you heard him," Ronan said.

"I'm not going until I find the well," Billy snapped.

The Captain stepped from the shadows. "Who votes to find the map for the little un?" he asked.

"Looks like you've been outvoted, Ronan," he smirked, as every one of the meadowers raised their hands.

"Finbar's nest is on the far side of the tunnel," the Captain whispered as he, Ronan and Tia dodged into the hidden recesses, avoiding the scurrying rat boys. Finbar's nest was a dome-shaped dungeon and, spying through its round window, Ronan spotted the treasure chest , its lid wide open, spilling the lavish jewels and trinkets onto the mucky ground.

"Wait a moment," the Captain warned, and, stopping Ronan and Tia with his arm, he sprang from the darkness and knocked a prowling rat boy flat on his hairy back.

"Go now," he hissed, and, producing a length of rope, he trussed the rat boy up like a chicken. "Don't worry, I'll keep an eye on this ugly critter," he grinned.

Ronan was a bit edgy. "It doesn't take two to look for a map," he snapped at Tia, prodding the trunk carefully with his sword, which he'd found under an orange flickering flame behind the arched door. Annoyed by his moodiness, and feeling queasy anyway from the smell of the rotten nest, Tia was happy to leave, giving the Captain a chance to rummage through his lost treasure.

"What's your problem, it's mine ain't it?" he growled, annoyed by Ronan's disapproving look.

"It's stolen!" Ronan scoffed.

"Yeah, that's what pirate's do. Like I said, it's mine. Now, stop acting like a sissy and look for the map, it won't bite ya," the Captain growled, and, stuffing his pockets with jewels, he grabbed Erin's wand and stepped outside.

Snoring behind a thick, red curtain, Ronan froze every time Finbar grunted.

"Ah, I think this is what we are looking for," he whispered, grabbing a dog-eared piece of parchment and dragging it from under a silver candlestick holder, as Finbar's snores raised the roof again.

"I found it," he said, acting more like his old self as he stepped outside. "It's not a man size map though," he said, rolling it up.

"Someone must have shrunk it, can't remember who for the life of me," said the puzzled Captain as they headed back down the long, damp tunnel.

"Bally bogs ahead," whispered the forest guardians, folding their wings having spotted the googly-eyed, fatheaded creatures pushing two disheveled figures around. And springing out of the blackness, Ronan landed a flying kick in one Bally bog's stomach and punched the other on the nose.

"They're out for the count," the Captain laughed, lifting their big eyelids and watching their eyes spinning like golf balls.

"Tia, is that you?" one of the disheveled figures asked, stepping into the light of the guardian's wings.

Tia was stunned. "King Marty, Queen Olivia!" she cried, rushing to embrace them.

"We should go now," said Ronan, trussing up the bally bogs.

"No, not yet, there are children locked in a room. Please, we can't leave them," said the King and Queen, beckoning them to come around the corner.

"It's useless, it's a man size door," said the Captain, listening to the children crying.

"Tia, try Erin's wand. Just make up any old rhyme, that's what she does," said Ronan, wiggling it around quite girlishly. Giggling, Tia waved the wand. *"Magic wand I implore – please open up the big stone door,"* she chanted and, to her surprise, the door flew open. A freckled faced, raggedy boy towered over them, and more raggedy boys and girls gathered behind him.

"Thank you," said the boy, blinking in disbelief at the tiny, wispy fairy with a wand in her hand, the tatty King and Queen, the pirate and the battered knight.

"Who locked you in here?" asked the Captain.

"It was the Dark Man, a shadowy figure in human form, he brought us here to slave for the rat boys," the boy told them.

"So, he's still around," said Erin,

"Thought he'd disappeared," said Ronan.

"The rat boys have found the treasure. Go quickly, go to the top, turn left, and keep going until you see a gap in the roof," said the Captain, pointing them in the right direction.

"What about you lot, aren't you coming too?" said a little girl, wiping the tears from her eyes.

"No, not yet," said Ronan. "We have a well to find."

"Keep running until you get home," called Tia, watching the raggedy children shinning happily over the rocks.

"Billy, we've found the map," whispered Tia, unlocking the stone door.

"Wicked," he squealed, lighting the lantern and staring at the two bedraggled strangers in tatty, green velvet cloaks.

"Er, who are they?" he asked.

"Mother! Father!" Erin screamed, throwing her arms around them.

"William, these are your great grandparents," she cried.

"Erin, I can't believe it's you," her father said, dabbing his eyes.

"What a handsome boy," her mother sobbed, squeezing Billy.

"We met a charming man with red hair, disguised as the Dark Man in the Forest of Darkness. He said you were searching for a healing well in the caves," the Queen cried, dabbing her eyes.

"We didn't believe it was you, but we had to find out," blubbed her father.

"This map is rubbish," Billy said, who, bored with the introductions and eager to find the well, rolled it out on the ground. Gathering behind him, they looked disappointedly at the three drawings, one of a waterfall, marked by an *X,* another of a small arch with '*Door*' written underneath, and a badly drawn key. Ronan flipped the parchment over to find another sketch on the back.

"Gran," Billy gasped, stabbing the parchment with his finger. "This is your locket – the key's inside," he said, gawping at the drawing of an oval shaped locket, the case open to reveal a key inside.

"But the locket's never opened," gasped Erin, even more amazed that Billy had called her Gran.

"Where's the locket now?" he yelled.

"Here," she said, unfastening it from around her neck and handing it to him.

"Where's the Captain?" he asked, spinning around. "He's in his room," the chorus of excited meadowers called, running after him.

"Captain Nealy, Captain Nealy, open up!" Billy screamed, banging the door with his fists.

"What in creation is going on? Do you want those fat rats to knobble us?" the peg-legged pirate hissed, grabbing Billy by the scruff of the neck.

"Look, Captain, is this the necklace the man gave to you?" he panted, dangling the locket.

"Yep, oval necklace," he read in his notes as Erin, Ronan, Patsy and Tia tumbled through the door.

"Where in the blue blazes did you find it?"

"It was a wedding present from William's Grand Pops. Do you know which farm you took it to, Captain?" Erin asked.

"Erm, it was Mcloughlin's farm," he barked, flicking the pages. "Now please, no more questions, I'm exhausted," he said, wondering why she was crying.

"I know exactly where that waterfall is," said Scruffy Tom, scratching his fluffy white beard, who, wearing a grubby blue bandana, was no scruffier than the others were.

"How do we get there?" Billy asked him eager to get going,

"It is time we used our secret route, and what better occasion," Scruffy Tom grinned.

"Fill your pockets, munchkins," the Captain chuckled, holding open the door to the jostling meadowers.

Tia unlocked the door with the stolen key, and filing through the pirates' ingenious route underneath the rat's nests which they had dug with their bare hands, they followed Scruffy Tom.

"You're in luck, there's not a single scraggy rat boy in sight," he whispered, pointing to where a waterfall trickled over the rocks.

"Where's Patsy? I need my last wish to reach the door, it'll be much easier if I'm a normal boy size," Billy said, seeing the faint outline of the arched door etched high up in the rock. And, scattering gold dust around Billy's feet, Patsy prayed that nothing would go wrong.

"Close ye're eyes and wish with all your heart, Billy boy," he said.

"Wait," said Erin rushing over and putting the locket in Billy's palm.

"Golden dust it would be Billy's greatest joy – if he could once more become a real boy," Patsy chanted dramatically, with a sweep of his hand.

"Ooooh," gasped the meadowers, as Billy stretched above them and, opening his eyes, he dangled the full-size locket over their heads.

Chapter 15

The Battle

"No!" Billy screamed, his hands batting away the swamp rats flapping wildly about his head. Snatching the locket, a swamp rat dropped it in between the rocks. Finbar scurried through the cave, a multitude of grey-cloaked rat boys trailing behind him cracking their long, black tails.

"Billy's search for the healing well wasn't a waste of time after all," Finbar bellowed, as Duke, with drool dribbling from the corner of his mouth, scampered to his side, a black bag gripped between his teeth.

"You surprise me, Captain Nealy. Don't you know that Ronan, the great guardian of Beltenor, is no friend of yours?" Finbar growled, snatching the wriggling bag from Duke. The Captain cocked his head to one side and stepped forward.

"Out with it, you hairy flea bag, what do you mean?" he barked.

Finbar hurled the sack without answering him, releasing a whistling black tornado that tore around the cave, blowing the meadowers off their feet. Then, breaking into several small, black clouds, they floated until each one was hovering over a pirate.

"Do you recognize them now, Ronan?" Finbar asked, practically dribbling with glee and, by the look on his face,

Billy knew that he did. The Captain and the pirates opened their mouths, and as each one swallowed the black cloud, they turned to look at Ronan with hatred in their eyes.

"Ronan cut your inner phantoms from you whilst you slept, hid them with the treasure, and you idiots buried them. That will teach you to steal from Beltenor, eh Ronan?" Finbar laughed, throwing a bundle of swords to the ground with a crash.

Pouncing, Captain Nealy snatched up his sword and, pointing it at Ronan, he charged.

"Out of my way or I'll run you through," he growled, and, pushing King Marty aside, he jabbed the sword at Ronan's throat.

"Captain, please, you and your crew are heroes. You ground the gold for the meadowers and if it weren't for you, William wouldn't be so close to finding the healing well. If you kill Ronan, it'll be what Finbar wants," Erin begged. The Captain took a step closer, still holding the sword to Ronan's throat.

"Heroes," he repeated, practically blushing. "Well, it's lucky for the tin soldier that we hate the rat boys even more. Don't worry, Ronan, you'll keep for another time," he growled. Changing his mind and swishing his sword, he charged at the rat boys, followed by his faithful, colourful crew. Relieved, Billy dropped to the ground and, grabbing the locket by the chain, he stuffed it in his pocket. Then, picking up a chunky piece of wood, he batted away the irritating swamp rats still flapping around his head.

Finbar leapt snarling from the rocks and, clamping his claw around Ronan's throat, he dragged him to the ground. Black tail flicking, fists flying and punching, scratching and biting they rolled around until they were exhausted. Then, bringing his foot up, Ronan kicked Finbar in his big, fat belly and at last, the winded rat boy keeled over. Fluttering, as well as scrambling, over the rocky surface, the meadowers rolled the biggest boulders they could find on top of the wriggling, squirming rat boys. Squealing in pain, Billy shook off a rat boy that clung to his thumb by its teeth and, swinging the wood, he saved the King and Queen from being carried away by the swamp rats. Patsy and Donal snatched up the dropped shillelaghs, clumped several rat boys and chased the cowardly bally bogs, who, with googly eyes rolling around in their sockets, scarpered into the tunnel.

Armed with their pockets full of gold dust, the leprechauns sprinkled it from a ledge. *"Golden dust float with ease –settle on the rats and make them freeze,"* they chanted, and drifting down, it froze them in their tracks.

Swishing their swords from side to side, Captain Nealey and his crew waded into the never-ending snarling rat boys that were still wriggling from every crevice.

Finbar opened his eyes again, and, spotting Ronan swinging his heavy sword, he staggered over the rocks and leapt on his back, knocking him down with his heavy frame. Then, dragging him to his feet, he hurled him against a rock with all his strength. Ronan slid to the ground with a clang and a small silver object fell to the ground with a chink. Pouncing on the silver whistle, Ronan blew it as hard as he could. A trumpet sounded from outside and, ears pricking up, a flurry of rat boys disappeared down the nearest hole.

"It will not make a sound but I will hear you," the Red-haired Man announced, sweeping through the roof on his winged black horse, followed by a band of ugly winged imps. Screeching like monkeys and gnashing their tomb stone teeth, the imps glided around the cave, sending the swamp rats flapping like a colony of bats and wily rat boys wriggling down the hill.

"I found the imps only recently. Looks like they'd been abandoned in the Forest of Darkness too," said the Red-haired Man, shaking Ronan's hand.

Billy could hardly believe it. The moment he'd dreamt of was here and, with everyone gathering around, he flicked open the locket. Taking out the tiny, gold key, he gasped as it grew in the palm of his hand. Then, slotting it into the keyhole, he turned it and opened the door. A bright light lit up the cave, and inside was a small well, brimming with sparkling, pure water.

"Wow," said Billy, dipping his sore thumb into the water and, with everyone clapping and cheering around him, he watched his wound heal. Then, picking up a crystal bottle nestling between the rocks, he filled it to the brim. "Thank you, St Kevin," he whispered, with tears in his eyes.

"You were meant to find the well, William," Erin said, fluttering to his side.

"I can't believe the key was around your neck all the time," he said. watching it shrink and then putting back it in the locket.

Erin stared at him for a moment, her green eyes misty. "William, I have to tell you something," she said, sounding very serious.

"What is it?" he asked, with a sinking feeling in the pit of his stomach.

"All those years ago when I became a mortal, the merrow told me, that should I return to Glendalough, I would remain a meadow fairy forever," she said, with a sob in her voice.

"What does that mean?" Billy asked, staring blankly.

"William, I can't go back, I have to stay here, as Erin the fairy queen," she whispered.

"No, I should never have run away. I can't lose you, Gran," he sobbed.

"You're not losing me, I'll always be here. Your mum is coming home, and you should be very proud," she said, the tears now shining in her eyes.

The next day at Dun Laoghaire (Dun Leery), it looked like every fairy in Ireland was there to see Billy off on the huge ferry. Leprechauns, pixies, gnomes, elves in red and green, meadow and marsh fairies, orange haired folk, forest guardians with blue wings buzzing frantically, and wispy tree spirits dabbing their eyes. Pleased that his ugly fish head had vanished with the discovery of the healing well, Ronan took off his tin helmet to show off his black gypsy curls. Captain Nealy and his crew, reunited with the ghost ship at last, were cheering under the billowing sails as they bobbed about on the sea, while above them, the beautiful Rainbow Bird swooped in and out of the fluffy clouds. The Red-haired Man, astride his black winged horse, saluted him as he sailed off into the clouds and, trying his best to smile, Patsy was blowing his nose on a big, spotted handkerchief. Except for Gran, Billy knew he would miss him most of all.

"Your dad will meet you at the port and take you straight to the hospital to see your mum, won't that be exciting? Be sure to tell her not to worry about me and that I'll be in touch," Erin said, wiping her eyes.

"How did you get my dad to come all the way from America?" Billy asked, smiling for the first time.

"Your dad knows that you need him, and I've told him I'm staying in Ireland until I'm well enough to travel," she winked. "Please, William, you must not be sad, I have work to do here and you've given your mum another chance. That's all that matters," she said, touching his face.

"You'll live forever, so that's cool," Billy said, choking back his tears.

"Never forget that you'll always be in here, for every second of every day," Erin said, and, with her hand over her heart, she hopped on to the Rainbow Bird.

"You too, Gran," Billy whispered, touching his chest.

"The meadow belongs to Queen Erin and the meadowers now," Ronan said, consoling a sobbing Tia, and, with a sudden jolt, her hand shot to her mouth.

"It's you, you're the mysterious Stranger," she gasped, her haunted eyes widening at the words she'd heard him speak so long ago.

"It's a long story, and I will explain," Ronan said, looking over his shoulder.

Up in the hills, the grass was rustling and Finbar and some of the whiskery rat boys poured from a hole in the ground to watch the touching little scene.

Standing on two legs Finbar looked through his binoculars. "So, he fooled us all, can you believe the Dark Man has been with us all along?" he rasped. And, lifting the binoculars again, he focused on Ronan's black gypsy curls.